Catfish Lullaby

Broken Eye Books is an independent press, here to bring you the odd, strange, and offbeat side of speculative fiction. Our stories tend to blend genres, highlighting the weird and blurring its boundaries with horror, sci-fi, and fantasy.

Support weird. Support indie.

brokeneyebooks.com
twitter.com/brokeneyebooks
facebook.com/brokeneyebooks
instagram.com/brokeneyebooks

Praise for

CATFISH LULLABY

"In her excellent novella, AC Wise revisits a Louisiana family at key moments during the later decades of the recent past—moments connected to what seems to be a local legend, one concerning the conflict between a pair of fantastical figures. Not only do her protagonists discover that what they took for fantasy is fact, they learn that it is more complicated than they could have expected. The result is a compelling narrative that begs to be read in one sitting." (**John Langan**, author of *Sefira and Other Betrayals*)

"Over the last few years, AC Wise has been consistently creating some of the very best speculative short fiction out there, and now with her glorious novella *Catfish Lullaby*, she takes her craft to a whole new level. With a potent atmosphere, a formidable antagonist, and well-drawn, unforgettable characters, this book has definitely got it all. An absolute must-read for 2019." (**Gwendolyn Kiste**, author of *The Rust Maidens* and *Pretty Marys All in a Row*)

"*Catfish Lullaby* seamlessly combines Southern folklore with cosmic horror. There's an elegiac undertone to this lullaby that's as deep and mysterious as the bayou where it takes place." (**Craig Laurance Gidney**, author of *A Spectral Hue*)

"Folk tales give birth to new mythologies in AC Wise's delightfully enthralling Southern Gothic novella *Catfish Lullaby*. Flooded with dark sorcery and white-knuckle suspense, *Catfish Lullaby* demonstrates the many ways saviors and devils can occupy the same body, whether it arises from the depths of the swamp or the dark of the grave." (**Mike Allen**, World Fantasy Award–nominated author of *Unseaming* and *Aftermath of an Industrial Accident*)

CATFISH LULLABY
by AC WISE

Published by
Broken Eye Books
www.brokeneyebooks.com

Cover illustration by Sishir Bommakanti
Cover design by Scott Gable
Interior design by Scott Gable
Editing by Scott Gable and C. Dombrowski

978-1-940372-29-7 (trade paperback)
978-1-940372-44-0 (ebook)

Catfish Lullaby

AC Wise

part 1

1986

There are stories about him along the Mississippi River from Cottonwood Point all the way down to New Orleans, maybe further still. Every place's got their own name for him—Wicked Silver, Old Tom, Fishhook—but where my people come from, smack dab in the middle of nowhere Louisiana, it was always Catfish John. Depending who you talk to, he's either a hero or a devil, one so wicked even hell won't take him.

—*Myths, History, and Legends from the Delta to the Bayou* (Whippoorwill Press, 2016)

Caleb lay facing the window, his grandmother's quilt pulled to his chin. From his position, he could just see the persimmon tree in the yard and, beyond it, the screen of pines separating his grandparents' property from Archie Royce's land. Back in the woods, past Royce's and where the ground started to go soft, Caleb's daddy—Lewis's sheriff—was leading a team to drag the swamp for a missing girl.

Caleb had heard Denny Harmon and Robert Lord talking about it at school. They were in first grade, but they'd probably both get held back, so Caleb would be stuck in the same class as them next year. Denny had said Catfish John took the girl.

"My cousin's friend was there. Catfish John came out of the swamp like a gator, mouth full of teeth. He grabbed her with his webbed hands and pulled her into the water."

Denny Harmon had grinned, looking like a gator himself, and looked right at Caleb.

"He probably killed her with a death roll and strung her up by her feet from the trees and slit her throat. He probably let her blood drain into the swamp to feed his catfish family."

Caleb hadn't run to tattle, but Robert held him while Denny punched him in the gut anyway, leaving him wheezing for breath.

"Catfish John likes sissy black boys best," Robert said, leaning close. "He'll leave us alone because we made it easier to catch you."

Mark, Caleb's best friend, found him after Denny and Robert left. Caleb's stomach hurt the rest of the day, but he still didn't tell. If Robert and Denny found out—and they would—it would only make things worse.

His stomach didn't hurt anymore, but he couldn't get Denny's words out of his head. His daddy was out in those woods. What if Catfish John got him? Even a sheriff with a gun could get eaten by a monster.

"I'm telling you who's responsible. Every damn fool in Lewis knows it 'cept nobody else is willing to do a thing about it." His grandfather's voice drifted under the bedroom door, interrupted by a nasty fit of coughing.

"Emmett, hush. Don't bring all that up again. 'Sides, you'll wake Caleb."

"Bet you he's awake anyhow." His grandfather chuckled, the rattling sound of his cough lingering.

Caleb started guiltily as his door opened, light from the hall spilling around his grandmother. It was too late to pretend he hadn't been listening.

"Can't sleep, sweet pea?" His grandmother didn't sound upset.

He sat up, nodding, and she sat on the edge of his bed. Caleb was surprised when his grandfather followed her into the room, crossing to the window to look out toward the trees.

"Did Catfish John kill somebody?" Caleb glanced between his grandparents.

His grandmother's mouth made a little *o*, and the skin around his grandfather's eyes crinkled like it did when he was mad—usually at the government buying up timber from people's land without paying a fair price.

"Damn ghost stories." He rested a hand on the window sill. Faint light showed a white scar across the back of his left hand, running from the knuckle of his first finger down to his wrist below his pinky. "That's what keeps folks from going after him. They think old Archie'll put a curse on 'em. Just like his daddy."

He sounded like he wanted to spit. Caleb sat up straighter. Did his grandfather think Archie Royce had something to do with the missing girl? There were stories about him too, though not as many as about Catfish John. Gators as big as trucks were supposed to guard Archie's property, and on top of that, the land was haunted on account of some people Archie's granddaddy killed a long time ago.

"What makes you ask about Catfish John?" His grandmother put her hand over Caleb's, her papery white skin a contrast to his warm brown.

Her look flickered past him to his grandfather. She smiled, but the expression went thin at the edges.

"I heard . . ." Caleb hesitated. If he told his grandmother about Robert and Denny, it might get back to them. His grandmother and Robert's nana both got their hair done at Miss Linda's place after all.

"Just something I heard at school." Caleb shrugged, looking down.

"Well, I know a story about Catfish John too." His grandmother leaned forward like she was about to tell a secret, and Caleb looked up again.

"Don't go filling his head with more nonsense, Dorrie." His grandfather spoke without turning from the window. He sounded more tired than upset.

"I want to hear," Caleb said.

"Well." His grandmother glanced at his grandfather, daring him to interrupt. When he didn't, she continued. "When I was little, my mama told me about a man who lived all alone in the swamp."

"Why?" Caleb caught himself too late, but his grandmother didn't fuss at him for interrupting like she normally would.

She smoothed the quilt. That must be why she was letting him stay up late; she was worried too.

"No one knows. There are a lot of stories about Catfish John. Some folks say he was chased out of his home by people who thought he was a bad man. They wanted to hurt him, and he ran into the swamp to hide. Now when my mama's best friend was a little girl, she got lost in the woods and wandered all the way to the swamp. She nearly drowned, but whatever reason he had for being there, Catfish John saved her life."

"But if he saved your mama's friend, then he'd be . . ." Caleb couldn't even begin to guess at his grandmother's mama's age. "He'd be a hundred years old, wouldn't he?" He looked at his grandmother to see if she was fooling him or if she'd smack his bottom for being rude.

"Maybe." She smiled, surprising him, and Caleb didn't see any sign of a trick.

By the window, his grandfather made a noise in his throat.

His grandmother kissed Caleb's forehead.

"Try to get some sleep, sweet pea. In the morning, I'll fix us all a big plate of 'nanner pancakes." She moved toward the door. "Come away from the window, Emmett. Your staring won't do any good."

His grandfather made another noise but followed his grandmother, closing the door behind him. Caleb tried to picture Catfish John saving a little girl. Maybe he'd help Caleb's daddy find the girl who was missing now. It was much a much nicer idea than the story Denny had told.

Caleb came awake to voices drifting from the hall, though he didn't remember falling asleep. Over the trees, the sky was a pearly grey. Not even dawn.

"No, but we found something else." Caleb focused in on his father's voice; he didn't sound happy.

"Might be Evaneen Milton, that girl down from Baton Rouge who disappeared six, seven years ago." His father's voice was rough with exhaustion. "There was barely anything left of her, but she had one of them medic alert bracelets."

"Oh, Charlie." His grandmother made a tutting noise. "Come on. I'll fix us some coffee." Their footsteps retreated down the hall.

Caleb sat up, fully awake now. They hadn't found the missing girl, but they'd found someone else, someone who'd gone missing before Caleb was even born. If that many people went missing in the swamp, maybe Denny was right after all. Maybe Catfish John did kill people, no matter what his grandmother said.

As he turned the thought over, a terrible sound split the air, echoing over the trees and making Caleb's skin pucker with goosebumps.

It was a snarling, wet sound. A scream that wasn't animal nor human but both. Like the swamp itself had found a voice, and it was angry that something that belonged to it had been taken away.

part 2

1992

chapter one

. . . nine feet tall, webbed hands, grey skin, mouth turned down at the corners, just like a catfish.

—*Myths, History, and Legends from the Delta to the Bayou* (Whippoorwill Press, 2016)

LATE AFTERNOON LIGHT HIT THE PERSIMMON TREE, SO THE FRUIT glowed, but all around, the grass was stained with a pattern like roots spread across the yard, a permanent, too-long shadow. Thin tendrils of black wrapped the tree's branches, and the leaves curled at the edges as though burned. Caleb plucked a fruit and pressed his thumb to the skin, black rot oozing from within. Dropping the fruit, he wiped his hand on his jeans.

"I've never seen anything like it." Caleb's father wiped an arm across his forehead, revealing half-moon circles of sweat staining his shirt. Early summer and already his skin bronzed brown-red from hours spent in the yard and on the porch under the eye of the sun.

"Whole thing's going to have to come out. Best burn the stump too, so it doesn't spread."

Caleb toed a blackened patch, half expecting it to smudge like ash, but it stayed put. The stain reminded him of something he couldn't place. Caleb half-listened to his father, thinking how his grandmother would have hated to see the tree go. Her persimmon jelly took the blue ribbon nearly every year at the Lewis County Fair.

"I'll go look for the chainsaw," his father said. "Once I get the tree down, I'll need your help hauling it."

Caleb nodded, and all at once, the nagging familiarity clicked into place. The rootlike pattern reminded him of the chest x-ray he'd glimpsed clipped to the chart at the foot of his grandmother's hospital bed, just before the end. She hadn't smoked a day in her life, but her lungs had been threaded with dark shadows. She'd outlived his grandfather but barely, and neither of them had been that old.

As his father disappeared around the side of the house, Caleb followed the shadows twisting away from the tree. They vanished in the pines bordering the property, headed toward Archie Royce's land. A flicker of movement between the trees made him start guiltily as though Archie Royce had caught him staring and now glared back.

Turning his back deliberately on the trees, Caleb pulled on work gloves and began gathering fallen persimmons. He chucked them into the garbage can they'd dragged into the yard, each exploding with a wet splat that was equal parts satisfying and unnerving. The back of his neck itched, and he fought the urge to turn around and see if he was actually being watched or if it was only his imagination. Even if it wasn't Archie Royce, that didn't mean nothing watched him.

Caleb shrugged, rolling his shoulders against the sensation. It struck him that he wasn't even sure what Archie Royce looked like. Lewis wasn't a big town, but even after all the years of his grandparents, and now him and his father, living just on the other side of the trees, Caleb had never seen their neighbor face to face.

There were plenty of rumors of course. One of his father's fishing buddies liked to tell a story about being chased off the Royce land with a shotgun when he was a kid. It could have been Archie Royce or his father, but whoever it was had fired into the air. From what he'd heard, with his skin, there was every chance Archie Royce would keep the gun level when he fired if Caleb ever strayed onto his land.

Archie wasn't the only mystery beyond the trees. Some folks said he had over a dozen kids—all by different women, not all of them willing—holed up on that property. Like his own private cult. Caleb had never seen evidence of them either. The only Royce he'd ever run into was Archie's son, Del. Even though Del looked old enough to be in college or be working at least, all he ever seemed to do was mooch around the Hilltop store, buying liquor and cigarettes. He'd broken in after hours once, but somehow, the charges hadn't stuck, and he'd been back on the streets of Lewis by the next day.

Caleb's main impression of Del was dark hair and a slouching walk. The closest Caleb had ever seen him was last summer when Caleb and Mark had gone to set pennies on the tracks for trains to flatten. Del had been crouched on the old track, running parallel to the new one, half its ties pulled up all the spaces between growing with weeds. At first, Caleb had thought Del was trying to light a fire, but then he'd heard the unmistakable scream of an animal in pain. Caleb had gotten just close enough to see what looked like a possum or a raccoon. Del had it staked to the tracks, his hands bloody like he was flaying it alive.

By the time Caleb and Mark had found someone to tell, it was too late. Del was gone, and he'd cleaned up all the evidence behind him.

"Hey. You hear me?" His father's voice jarred Caleb back to the present.

"Sir?" Caleb realized he was standing with a handful of rotten persimmons, staring into the trees despite himself.

"I said, why don't you start in on the branches with these clippers. I'm going to have to run into Buck's for a new chain. This one's rusted through."

"Yessir." Caleb accepted the clippers his father held out.

After a moment, the truck's engine roared to life. Caleb squeezed the handles of the clippers together, and the branch between the blades gave with a dry snap like breaking bone.

Sweat gathered as he worked, his muscles aching pleasantly. Even so, he couldn't help pausing every now and then to glance at the trees. His grandfather talked about Archie's father, Clayton, sometimes, but more often than not, Caleb's grandmother would shush him. Still, it was pretty clear his grandfather hadn't liked the man.

There was a plaque at town hall dedicated to a Reverend Elphias Royce. The family had been in Lewis for generations; they'd practically founded the town, but for all that, no one really seemed to like them as far as Caleb knew. Over the years, the family had grown increasingly reclusive, and the rumors about them nastier. But that's all it was, rumors. Nothing legal stuck, just like Del breaking into Hilltop. It was like the family and even the land had some supernatural force around it.

Caleb gathered the cut branches and dumped the armload in the trash on top of the burst fruit. The black goo in the bottom of the can smelled foul, and Caleb regretted busting them. Burning the tree stump didn't seem like such a bad idea after all. He pictured the flames following the black lines of rot all the way back to Archie Royce's house. Maybe that wouldn't be such a bad thing either.

Caleb woke to ruddy light blazing above the tree line, bright as dawn but the wrong color. His first sleep-muzzed thought was that his father had decided to burn the stump after all. But that would be a controlled burn and not in the middle of the night. He rocketed up, rushing down the hall to bang on his father's door.

"Caleb, what—" His father's eyes were red with exhaustion; insomnia often ate away his hours until late into the night. He'd probably only just gotten to sleep.

"Archie Royce's place is burning." A sick thrill ran through Caleb. Hadn't he wished that very thing?

Coming awake all at once, his father reached for the phone on the nightstand, twisting the cord around as he gathered his shirt and boots, dressing as he talked. When he hung up, his expression was grim.

"What's wrong?"

His father shook his head, throwing a flannel work shirt over his T-shirt, leaving his boots unlaced.

"Gerry March says it'll take him half an hour to rouse a crew and get over here. That's bullshit." A muscle in his father's jaw twitched. "Archie's got kids in there."

The words sparked guilt over the strange thrill Caleb had felt. Thoughts weren't actions but still.

"The fire won't come over the trees." His father moved toward the door. "If it does, you take the old truck down the road to Ginny Mason's place, and you stay there. You hear?"

"I want to help." Caleb spoke before his brain had time to catch up with his mouth.

His father stopped so abruptly Caleb almost crashed into him.

Even if his father wasn't Lewis's sheriff, he'd still help Archie Royce, no matter what he thought of him. Because it was the right thing to do. Caleb knew he wasn't really to blame just because he'd imagined a fire, but his father's words and his own willingness to help still left him with a feeling of responsibility. Whatever the truth about Archie Royce might be, if he did have kids in there—Del aside—they didn't deserve to die. Caleb stood straighter, adrenaline surging and mixing with his nerves as his father looked him over.

"All right. Let's go."

As his father stepped outside, Caleb's legs turned briefly to rubber; he hadn't expected his father to agree. The truck's engine roared, and headlights flooded the yard. Caleb hurried to catch up.

Caleb's chest remained tight as his father steered onto the main road. The night was silent. No wail of sirens. If their house had been the one burning, trucks would be on the way by now, but because it was Archie Royce's place, Gerry March was content to make excuses and let it burn.

The idea dug at Caleb. No one in Lewis ever took direct action against the Royces, but it seemed they wouldn't take direct action to save them either. He scrabbled for purchase as his father turned hard, slewing the truck onto a barely visible drive. His teeth clicked together as the wheels jounced in worn ruts until his father brought the truck to a halt.

Whip-thin trees framed the burning house. They looked sicker than the persimmon his father had cut down, leaning away as though trying to escape. But if the persimmon was any indication, the trees would be hell to cut down, even diseased. If the fire touched them, would they even burn?

Despite being engulfed, Caleb could see the Royce house had once been grand. He and Mark had never been invited to joyride down the roads at night when other kids from school dared each other onto the property. Seeing the place now, Caleb was glad.

His father climbed out of the truck, leaving the sharp sting of smoke to drift through the open door. Caleb opened his own door and went to stand by the hood.

A beam popped deep in the house, and a section of roof collapsed, sending up a rush of sparks. Caleb lifted his shirt over his nose and mouth. The brightness made a hard backlight to shapes directly in front of the house—a junked car, the remains of a well, and closer to the house, an odd-shaped blot. It took Caleb's eyes a moment to adjust, and even then, his mind didn't want to agree. A girl, standing far too close to the flames.

"Dad!"

His father hoisted his own shirt over his nose and mouth as Caleb pointed.

The air wavered, weirdly thick around the girl. It wasn't just the heat rolling off the place; his father moved as though wading through waist-deep water. She didn't react when his father reached her. When he took her by the shoulders, steering her toward the truck, she didn't resist either.

"Get a blanket from the back," his father called, and Caleb hurried to obey.

"Take care of her. I'm going to see if there's anyone else."

His father wrapped the blanket around the girl's shoulders and gave her a gentle nudge in Caleb's direction. Caleb watched him walk back toward the flames. The girl's attention remained fixed on the house. He couldn't imagine watching everything he'd ever known burn—his bed, his baseball trophies, the picture of his mother and father and him as a baby sitting on a big striped blanket on the front lawn.

"I'm Caleb." Introducing himself felt stupid given the situation, but if he could get her talking, maybe it would distract her. He lowered the shirt from his mouth. "What's your name?"

The girl ignored him. Caleb looked at her more closely. Smoke and ash streaked her pale skin. Out of nowhere, an odd thought struck Caleb like something coming up out of the swamp. He'd never heard of a woman living at Archie Royce's place; the rumors said all his kids had different mothers who no one ever saw. What if the body his father had found in the swamp all those years ago was this girl's mother?

There was a thinness to her like hunger but deeper. Below the blanket, her feet were bare. She looked about his age, but it was hard to tell. She was at least a head shorter than him, but Caleb was tall for his age. His limbs had been called gangly, and hers had the same thinness but without the awkwardness of knobby elbows and knees that didn't fit.

She clutched something close against her body like she was afraid someone would take it. Caleb could just make out what looked like a figurine roughly the size of a baseball, carved from dark wood. Except when he looked closer, the wood took on a reddish hue, streaked with dark bands like smoke. And as he watched, the bands grew, staining the wood pure black. The reflected firelight must have been messing with his sight.

He blinked, focusing on the girl's face instead.

"Are you okay?"

Another stupid thing to say. Of course, she wasn't. He touched her shoulder. She jerked away, startled, but finally turned to face him. Even though the firelight was behind her, her eyes seemed to glow for a moment, and a faint light shone from her skin too. Then the girl blinked, and her eyes were just a normal muddy green-brown. Except she wasn't crying. That struck Caleb as odd. Her house was burning, and there were no tracks in the soot smearing her cheeks.

"Hey . . ." Spooked, Caleb let the word trail.

The girl pivoted on her bare heels, and for a moment, Caleb feared she would sprint back into the burning house. Instead she spat in the dirt at her feet. A sound like the one he'd heard the night his father pulled the bones from the swamp, a sound Caleb would never forget—sorrow and rage—split the air.

Caleb's skin prickled, but movement at the corner of his eye caught his attention. The smoke above the house shifted. As Caleb stared, it formed a face, impossible but distinct and inhuman. The night sky howled again, and beside him, the girl went rigid. Her fingers curled tight around the carving, her lips pulling back from her teeth. Then her head whipped around, a dog scenting deer.

Caleb squinted, trying to see what she saw. A blot of darkness, like she'd been at first, but larger. A man stood near the side of the house, but there was something wrong about his shape.

The girl lurched toward the fire. Instinctively Caleb threw his arms around her to hold her back. Her body hitched like a sob, but the noise that emerged was a keening cry. It was almost music, raw and laced with rage, and it made lightning crawl under Caleb's skin.

The sound went on, a contrast to the wet, red sound howling above the house. The girl's throat worked, reminding Caleb of a pelican struggling with a fish. The noise coming out of her looked painful.

She strained forward again, throwing him off balance. They crashed to the ground, dust billowing around them, adding to the smoke and making Caleb cough. The girl was a knot of sinew, wild and thrashing. Caleb caught her wrists to keep her from hitting him.

All at once, she went still, her breath shallow. Her eyes reflected the light from the house. Burning. Except the angle was wrong, the light behind her. Caleb let go of her wrists with a shout, her skin suddenly hot.

The wail of sirens cut the night, far too late, and the girl slumped, the fight gone. Caleb scrambled to stand. Adrenaline shook him; it was a moment before he caught his breath, a moment longer before he could string together a coherent thought. He got his hands under the girl's armpits and hauled her to her feet.

"I couldn't find anyone else." Caleb's father returned, his voice worn hollow as his expression.

He frowned as though he couldn't quite remember how Caleb and the girl had gotten there. As the fire engine finally pulled into the drive, his expression changed, going flint hard. Caleb watched his father stride toward the splash of red and white lights, ready to give Gerry March hell. When the girl spoke beside him, Caleb jumped.

"Cere."

"What?" Caleb stared at her.

Her voice was smoke-rough, a croak. Light no longer burned in her eyes. Where they'd been muddy green-brown before, they now appeared green-grey like pale moss clinging to a stone.

"Cere." She fixed on him in a way that brought back the electric fizzing beneath his skin. Caleb let out a breath, realizing she'd finally offered him her name.

Cere perched on the edge of a kitchen chair, hands wrapped around a mug of coffee she'd barely touched. She wore clothes one of the nurses at the hospital had found her—jeans and a ringer T-shirt with Lewis High's bronco in maroon against white.

"Cere's going to stay with us for a while until things get sorted out." Caleb's father put a hand on Caleb's shoulder.

Caleb nodded, but his gaze kept sliding back to Cere. She'd barely acknowledged either of them, not that he could blame her.

"Caleb." His father shook him lightly. "Are you listening?"

"Yessir." The words slid out automatically.

"Good. I have to go make some more calls." There were shadows under his eyes.

It had been a long night, from the fire to Deer Creek Hospital and back here. None of them had slept. Under the kitchen light, away from the smoke and fire, Caleb finally had a chance to get a good look at Cere. Her hair was an odd blonde that was almost silvery. The nurse had worked it into two thick braids that hung over her shoulders. Even for a white girl, she was pale, her wrists showing the faint blue blush of her veins. The pallor was offset by a shock of freckles scattered across her cheeks and nose like a constellation. On top of that, Caleb still couldn't get a good fix on the color of her eyes, which seemed to shift constantly.

Caleb poured himself a bowl of cereal. He placed the box close enough that Cere could reach it if she wanted and then sat at the far end of the table. Cere didn't raise her head. From the far end of the hall, Caleb heard the murmur of his father's voice. He'd been on the phone for hours, trying to track down any other members of Cere's family, but the set of his jaw told Caleb everything he needed to know about how little enthusiasm he had for finding anyone with the last name Royce.

Caleb took a bite of his cereal, finding it tasteless. Within the span of twenty-four hours, less, the world had been turned completely upside down. After Gerry March's team had gotten the fire under control, they'd found Archie Royce's remains in the burned-out shell of the house. Caleb had heard his father mention someone named Ellis who must be another of Cere's brothers. He hadn't heard anything about Del, and it wasn't clear whether their bodies had been found or whether there'd been anyone else in the house.

Cere kicked her heels against the rung of her chair, a restless drumming sound. Caleb abandoned his spoon. The one bite he'd taken already felt like a solid lump in his stomach.

"Do you like baseball?" It was the only thing he could think to say.

Cere raised her head. Ignoring her unsettling eyes, Caleb plowed on.

"Our team was pretty good last year. We went all the way to regional finals. Then Coach Stevens left, and now we suck."

Anything to fill the silence. Cere didn't blink. There was something wrong with her eyes beyond their shifting color. Subtle threads of gold bled into them from the edges. It made Caleb think of the black shadows on the lawn but in reverse.

Caleb shoved his chair back, dumped the rest of his cereal into the sink. To his surprise, Cere followed him down the hall, a pale shadow. He was too stunned to close the door before she slipped past him into his room.

"What are you—"

Cere glanced over her shoulder, stilling him. Caleb held his breath as she trailed her fingers over the bedspread, taking in his books, his trophies, his bat and glove leaning against the closet door. Her hand rested on the photograph of him as a baby with his parents and something coiled tight inside him.

He'd been so young when she died. The picture was the only way he could remember what his mother looked like. He would stare, trying to fix every feature in his mind—her hair carefully smoothed and curled, her skin several shades darker than his, but her eyes just like his own. When he looked at the picture, he could almost remember her laugh, the sound of her voice as she moved around the kitchen while he played on a blanket spread on the floor. Then it would slip again, and her face would blur. Those moments of forgetting were his own personal experience of loss. It was like remembering her death, even though he hadn't fully experienced it at the time. If Cere damaged the picture . . .

He moved to snatch the frame out of her hand as Cere turned her head without moving the rest of her body. It made Caleb think of a bird. Her eyes, the color of Spanish moss now, pinned him, and Caleb's breath stuttered. The gold threads within her irises were unmistakable; they squirmed. She tapped the picture's frame. Everything he'd been feeling uncoiled into guilt. His parents smiling, Caleb between them, a happy family. Even if he'd lost part of it, it must still be more than she'd ever had.

Cere lowered her hand. She turned fully now, facing him. Her voice was still a smoke-rough whisper, every bit as startling as it had been last night.

"I was born to end the world."

Caleb woke with his heart pounding, convinced the sky was on fire on the other side of the trees. But only stars shone above the pine and oak. Vents sighed with a sudden rush of chill from the air conditioning, and Caleb tugged his blanket higher. Fragments of a dream clung to him. A fat ball of flaming gold crawling into the sky and a great frog or a fish swallowing it whole. There had also been something with scales diving into muck and a woman walking between cypress knees. Her bare feet splashed in shallow water, and she cradled her swollen belly. She glowed.

I was born to end the world.

Even as the images faded, certainty clung to him that the woman in his dream was Cere but older, and the thing she carried in her belly wasn't a child; it was something terrible, darkness and fire, a thing too big to wrap his mind around.

Caleb pressed his ear to the wall dividing his room from Cere's. He was startled to hear a faint murmur, what sounded like "please." The wall under his ear felt hot, the skin of the house glowing like the woman in his dream. He jerked back but not before he heard her window sliding up.

Caleb reached his own window just in time to see a shadow dart across the lawn. Cere. He knew he should tell his father, but at the same time, he couldn't help thinking about the way Cere's eyes squirmed with gold. If she chose to run away, that wasn't his problem. Caleb tried to convince himself, tried to ignore the hammer of his pulse telling him otherwise. He pulled the covers over his head. He was still dreaming; he hadn't seen anything at all.

chapter two

. . . a preacher walking along the road met a devil. Or maybe he met another preacher. It's not important. That's not the point of the story. In fact, it isn't really a story. It's an excuse for two people to talk about different kinds of philosophy and religion and which one's better. At the end, it turns into a story again. After all their good conversing and friendly debating, the preacher and the devil disagree, and the disagreement comes to blows. When they part ways, both of them bloodied, the preacher swears he'll destroy the devil one day. Even if it takes him and his children and his children's children to the end of the earth to do it.

—*Myths, History, and Legends from the Delta to the Bayou* (Whippoorwill Press, 2016)

"Nothing else was taken? Only . . . shit, yeah, that's bad enough."

Caleb stopped in the kitchen doorway. His father's back was turned, the phone trapped between his shoulder and his ear as he scribbled in a pocket-sized notepad.

"Okay. I'll be there as soon as I can." His father hung up, and it was too late to pretend he hadn't overheard.

"What happened?" Caleb wasn't sure where to look, certain his father would read his guilt. Something bad had happened to Cere, or she'd done something bad. He should've woken his father when he saw her run away.

"Someone broke into the morgue last night." Caleb's father rubbed a weary palm over his face. The words caught Caleb by surprise. "Probably kids on a stupid dare."

The same thing had happened a few years back; his father had arrested three Lewis High seniors trying to break into the morgue. But his father had said "broke into" not "attempted." And something had been taken.

Archie Royce's body was in that morgue.

"Damn. Cere sure makes a good cup of coffee."

"Huh?" Caleb started but shut his mouth.

"She was up hours before you." His father waved his mug toward the doorway, and Caleb turned to see Cere freshly dressed in clothes that actually fit. Maybe he had dreamed her running away after all.

"First day of school. Big day. I know there's barely two weeks left in the year, but I pulled some strings."

His father smiled, but the strain showed behind it. Getting Cere into school right before summer vacation probably had more to do with getting her out of the way—her and Caleb both—and that made her Caleb's problem again. Caleb glanced at her. *Could* she have had something to do with the break in?

"Bus'll be here soon. Better get going." Caleb's father didn't leave room for objections.

As the bus pulled up to their drive, a new worry struck Caleb. Gossip would already have made its wildfire circuit around Lewis. Half the kids on the bus, if not all, would know about Cere.

Caleb hunched his shoulders under his backpack as he hurried down the drive, not bothering to see if Cere kept up. He looked at his feet as he climbed on board and headed toward the back. Silence followed, which was almost worse than whispers. He had the urge to shove Cere away from him. He didn't need any more reason for Robert Lord and Denny Harmon to pick on him. Not that they ever needed an excuse.

Halfway back, Mark Nayar waved Caleb to the seat beside him. Mark's parents were born in India; as the only two non-white kids in their class—in practically the whole school—they'd gravitated toward each other the first day of kindergarten. The friendship had stuck.

Unlike Caleb, Mark had an amazing ability to shrug off the whispers and name-calling. Mark was one of the smallest boys in their class, but he hardly ever got beat up. The way he grinned and shrugged in response to attempts to bait him probably made Robert and Denny uneasy. It was easier to pretend he didn't exist. Which left Caleb—and no matter how many times he tried to follow Mark's example, he couldn't seem to grow his skin as thick.

Caleb slid into the seat in front of Mark, leaving space for Cere to sit beside him. *Be like Mark. Stick by Cere. Don't let them get to you.* Caleb recited the mantra in his head, holding himself rigid. Mark leaned over the seat between them and stuck out his hand.

"I'm Mark." Cere regarded him coolly, and Caleb braced himself for her to say something weird. To his surprise, Cere took Mark's hand, blinking her expression into one of mild politeness.

"Hello." They shook hands, and Caleb felt some of his tension unwind, but it didn't last long.

As the bus wheezed forward, a chewed wad of paper, soaked in spit, hit the back of Cere's head. From the telltale hyena laughter, Caleb didn't have to turn to know Robert and Denny were to blame. A second wad struck Cere's head, followed by a stage whisper.

"Hey, witch-bitch. Swamp girl."

Very slowly, Cere turned around.

"Don't." Caleb's throat tightened on the hypocrisy of the word. Robert and Denny had left him with countless bruises over the years, always placed just so they could be plausibly explained as an accident during baseball. "They're not worth it."

"Hey, you guys want to hear a good joke?" Mark knelt on his seat, facing Robert and Denny.

"Shut it, Nayar."

Mark ignored Denny, launching into a long setup Caleb recognized from an old Bill Hicks routine. Mark was determined to be a stand-up comedian someday and spent hours memorizing routines. Caleb hunched his shoulders higher. Maybe Mark's joke would distract them. Maybe not. The words *faggot* and *queer* bounced around in his head, and he curled his fingers around the edge of the cracked vinyl seat.

"Yes. I am a witch." Cere's voice, near toneless, cut across Mark's words, and he fell silent, his mouth dropping open.

Cere knelt on the seat now too, looking straight at Robert and Denny. The shirt she wore—who knows where his father had found it—finally registered: the Care Bears lined up under a glittering rainbow stretched over puffy clouds. Nervous laughter clogged Caleb's throat, turning into a cough.

"What are you going to do, witch-bitch?" Robert found his voice, but his gaze cut left, looking for support from Denny. "Put a spell on us?"

"Maybe."

Cere pointed at Robert's chest. Her eyes rolled back, crescents of white showing beneath her lids, and she mumbled words Caleb couldn't make out. His chest tightened, unreasonable fear. Her skin wasn't glowing; there were no threads of gold in her eyes. But still.

"You'd better fucking stop it." Robert's eyes widened.

Cere ignored him, her voice going lower, almost a growl.

"I'm warning you," Robert said, he stood up halfway.

The bus driver, Mrs. Reeves, smacked the horn. "Sit down while the bus is moving."

Robert slouched low, arms crossed, scowling. Cere returned to her original position, sitting straight with her hands in her lap. The faintest of smiles touched her lips, the first Caleb had seen from her. A whoop built in his chest; he wanted to punch her shoulder in victory, but a flickering hint of pain in her eyes stopped him. She looked much older than twelve, making Caleb think of the woman in his dream. Mark leaned over the seat between them.

"What was that? What did you do to him?"

Now Cere's smile was unmistakable, even though the shadows didn't leave her eyes.

"Nothing. I was just saying 'rhubarb, rhubarb, rhubarb.'"

"Huh?" Mark looked confused, but Caleb couldn't help but grin—part appreciative and part embarrassed. He'd almost believed Cere's performance. He nudged her with his elbow.

"That was great."

Her smile faded, and she knotted her hands together in her lap. Her reply was so soft, Caleb wasn't sure Mark was meant to hear. Or him for that matter.

"Sometimes you have to be scarier than the monsters."

chapter three

Ask anyone, they'll tell you this area is haunted. Maybe they don't believe in ghosts, but they know someone who has a story—weird lights in the trees, strange music, a shadowy figure that disappears when you look head-on. There are empty places here, lonely stretches with more trees than people. Sure there are old forests out West and big open spaces in the Midwest, but it's not the same. In the South, we have our own blood and pain, and time moves different here. People from elsewhere say folks talk slower down here. We're slower to forget too and slower to forgive. Even the land holds onto its scars.

Small towns like this, folks'll give you the shirt off their backs and then turn right around, talk about you when you're gone. That doesn't make them any less kind or good. It's just the way things are. See, there are two Souths: one on the surface, one underneath. Underneath is where we keep our angels and our demons both.

—*Myths, History, and Legends from the Delta to the Bayou* (Whippoorwill Press, 2016)

LIGHT GLINTED OFF THE WATER. CALEB GRIPPED THE ROPE SWING AND balanced one foot on the knot near the bottom before kicking off. The creek was swollen high, but there was still a fluttering moment of stomach-dropping fear as he let go. He tucked his limbs and let out a whoop, pinching his nose just before he struck the water.

Cold slapped him, waking every part of his skin, but he had enough experience not to gasp and pull water into his lungs. He'd been jumping off this swing almost since he could walk. Bubbles rose around him, guiding him as he kicked back to the surface.

Mark perched on one of the big boulders on the shore. The last two weeks of classes had unrolled in a blur. There hadn't been another incident with Cere since the first day on the bus. The most dramatic thing that happened was Mark breaking his arm on a dare, jumping off the slide. He waved his cast-bound arm now and lobbed a pinecone with his free hand, so Caleb had to duck under the water to avoid it.

"Outta my way, asswipe." Denny grabbed the rope swing as Caleb surfaced again.

He pulled himself onto the muddy bank as Denny cannonballed into the creek, spraying water. The first day of summer, the first day of freedom. He wouldn't let Denny spoil his mood. Even Mark was having fun, despite the cast. Caleb clambered onto the boulder beside him, leaving damp patches that evaporated quickly in the sun.

"Hey, faggot."

Caleb's head snapped up, immediately hating himself for the reflexive motion. Denny snickered, standing ankle-deep in the water.

"Ignore him." Mark nudged Caleb as Denny kicked at the water, sending up a spray that fell short of their perch.

"Where's your girlfriend?"

"I don't have a girl—" Caleb stopped, feeling the trap too late. The light in Denny's eyes shifted. Robert waded over to join him, standing shoulder to shoulder, their expressions identical and cruel.

"The witch-bitch," Denny said, elbowing Robert. "Bet she likes dark meat."

"Fuck off." Caleb stood, the words out before he could stop them.

His skin prickled. There was no Mrs. Reeves now, no adults at all to stop Denny and Robert. There was no one to stop him either.

"Come down here and make me, nigger." Robert narrowed his eyes, speaking the last word like candy on his tongue. His smile spread, melting butter, and Caleb's skin went from hot to cold, the word landing like a punch to the gut.

Between the two, Robert was more dangerous. It was one of Lewis's open secrets that Robert's granddaddy had been part of the Klan, and his robe and pointy hood were still in a box somewhere in Robert's daddy's garage.

Caleb jumped down, feet squelching in the creek mud. He was at least of a height with Denny and taller than Robert, but they each had a good ten pounds on him. This was suicide.

"Let it go." Mark was on his feet now too. Caleb ignored him.

Where *was* Cere? What if Robert and Denny had done something to her?

"What did you do to her?" The sun hit Caleb's eyes. He squinted.

"More like what did *you* do to her? You take a look at her little titties in the shower, or are you too much of a fag?" Now it was Denny's turn again. He snickered at his own joke, and beside him, Robert continued to watch Caleb with half-lidded eyes, making Caleb think of a snake. Not a rattler that announced its presence with bluster and sound, more like a cottonmouth, silent until it struck.

"Lookit the faggot get mad." Denny elbowed Robert again.

Caleb's fingers curled. The words stung, clinging to him like a second skin.

"Fuck you!" Caleb shoved Robert as hard as he could, and Robert took a step to keep his balance.

"Caleb, don't." Mark scrambled down from the boulder, awkward with one arm. At that moment, Denny's fist slammed into Caleb's stomach.

He folded, and the world went grey-black with pain. He heard Mark shout, but Caleb could only wheeze, curling around the point of impact. Robert tackled him, and Caleb went down. When he tried to roll away from the pain, Robert kicked him. Caleb tasted blood.

Through the haze, he was vaguely aware of other kids gathering, but no one moved to help. He hauled in a ragged breath, coughing, and got one arm beneath him. Denny kicked him in the elbow, dropping Caleb back into the mud where he flopped like a landed fish.

"Get up and fight." Robert nudged Caleb with his toes, his voice hungry.

Caleb managed to lift his head just as a pair of fish-pale hands snaked out of the water and clamped around Robert's ankles, yanking. Instead of going to his knees, Robert tipped straight forward like a felled tree, his stomach striking the muddy shore with a painful slap. His breath left him in a grunt, which turned into a strange high-pitched squeal.

Caleb scrambled back. A piglet had escaped from Roy Wilson's last summer and got tangled in barbed wire; it had made the same sound.

Robert clawed at the shore, fingers scoring furrows in the mud as something dragged him backward. Water lapped his knees, his hips, his chest; his eyes went panic-wide. Cere popped out of the water behind him, grinning. Denny huffed out a breath of surprise. Even though Cere no longer held him, Robert continued to thrash for a moment before slumping still, tremors running up and down his body in a series of aftershocks.

"She killed him," Denny shouted. "The witch-bitch killed him."

A line of blood snaked from Robert's nose. Denny leapt toward Cere. She ducked under the water, and Denny slipped, going down with a heavy splash. He came up spluttering, dove again, and surfaced empty-handed. It was almost comical, watching Denny's face getting redder. But the fact that Robert hadn't moved, hadn't blinked, and the blood running from his nose left Caleb cold.

Before Caleb could touch him to check, Robert leapt straight up. He wiped at the blood running from his nose, smearing it across his cheeks and chin.

"Are you okay?" Caleb stood, ignoring the pain, but Robert spun on his heel and sprinted up the path toward the road.

Caleb stared after him. Stunned silence spread around the creek, followed by a ripple of whispers. He heard "witch" and "spell" and "curse."

Cold fingers brushed Caleb's palm, and he jumped. Cere stood behind him as though she'd just stepped out from the trees. Her braids were dark with water, dripping over her shoulders.

"What did you do?" Caleb wasn't sure if he was asking what she'd done to Robert to make him scream, make his nose bleed, or how she'd managed to drag him when he easily weighed fifteen pounds more than her. Or how she'd disappeared under the water and reappeared behind him in the woods.

Cere's grin faded, her eyes going a muddy-dark like pain.

"I saved you," she said.

Caleb shook his head. Under the leaf shadows, she barely looked human. A witch-bitch, just like Robert and Denny said. He was sharply aware of the others, even Mark, staring at them.

"Let's go." He shooed Cere ahead of him, touching her only with the tips of his fingers.

More whispers followed them, and Caleb hurried his steps. He caught Cere's arm, his fingers making a dark bracelet around her upper arm. At the road, she stopped hard, refusing to move.

"I saved you." Her voice was louder now. Caleb let go, but she leaned closer, glaring. "I can't always keep the dark inside. All I did was let him see."

All at once, Caleb's anger went out of him. He had no idea what she was talking about, but he could see the way she shook. It was like she was trying to hold something back. Even in the bright sunlight, her shadow loomed bigger than her. She was Cere, and then she wasn't. She was . . . *something*. Bits of her slid in and out of focus, and Caleb couldn't put the pieces together. His mind reeled, and he stepped back. Then all at once she snapped back into place, looking smaller than she had even before, lost and hurting.

"I'm sorry." Caleb rushed the words.

Cere's mouth opened; she looked like she hadn't expected an apology, had never heard one before. They stared at each other, waiting. Caleb swallowed. Cere *had* helped him, though he hadn't given her any reason. Who knows how far Denny and Robert would have gone if she hadn't stopped them.

"Thank you."

If felt inadequate. He wanted to say more, something comforting, but the words wouldn't come. Cere nodded, her lips pressed into a thin line. The tension evaporated, and she resumed walking; the dull ache from Denny and Robert's blows caught up with him, and Caleb limped after her.

Caleb's father held out a plastic baggie filled with ice. "Wanna tell your side of the story?"

Caleb didn't. The split in his lip wasn't deep enough for stitches, but it throbbed, and the first touch of cold on the swollen skin made him suck in a sharp breath. His father leaned against the kitchen counter, arms crossed.

"I got a call from Angeline Lord. Robert claims you tried to drown him."

Caleb pressed the ice down harder, welcoming the pain.

"Look." His father sighed; Caleb didn't hear anger, just weariness. "I know you don't start fights. And I wouldn't trust that Lord boy as far as I could throw him. His daddy's no good, and he's got the same mean streak, but that's no excuse."

"He called me . . ." Caleb stopped, lowered the ice.

His lips felt numb now, and that almost made the words easier; he could pretend someone else was talking.

"Robert said the N-word." Caleb hesitated. He knew his father had heard the word a thousand times about his wife, about his son. It felt strange, softening it, but it would be equally wrong saying it out loud.

"And he called me . . ." Here Caleb stopped, and his stomach clenched. Saying the other word—Robert and Denny's favorite word for him—felt almost worse, like admitting something. If he said it out loud, it would be true. *Faggot.* He took a deep breath.

"Denny and Robert are assholes." Caleb drew himself up straight. Maybe he would get in trouble for saying it, but it was the truth.

He braced himself, expecting a lecture. His father had never once whupped him like he suspected Denny Harmon's daddy did to him. But words could be worse; words left guilt gnawing its way around inside Caleb, knowing he'd let his father down when he already had so much to deal with: work and raising Caleb alone now that his grandparents were gone. And now Cere too.

Instead of a lecture, so flickering brief he might have imagined it, Caleb saw his father struggle with a smile. He gaped, but remembering himself, he launched into the speech he'd practiced on the walk home. If he got it out quick enough, it wouldn't be a lie. The whole truth was he *didn't* know what happened, not really.

"Robert and Denny were saying bad things about Cere. I tried to get them to stop, and Robert punched me. We fought, and Robert must've got tangled somehow in the water and freaked out. Maybe he was embarrassed, so he said I tried to drown him."

Caleb forced himself to meet his father's eyes. He tried hard not to see Robert shivering in the mud, blood leaking from his nose. Denny and the others could call him a liar. Mark might back him up, but even he'd looked scared of Cere.

I saved you. The words echoed in Caleb's head. He couldn't rat Cere out, not after seeing the look in her eyes. It hurt her, helping him, and he owed her.

His father looked away first, surprising Caleb. He *wanted* to believe Caleb, which made it worse. The rest of his story, the part Caleb didn't understand—where Cere could hold her breath, disappear and reappear somewhere else, where her shadow didn't fit her body—sat heavily in his throat.

"See this?" His father pushed back his hair, revealing a faint scar. "Buck Harmon gave me that in third grade."

His father let his hair fall back into place.

"As for Bobby Lord, he called your mama the N-word once too. You know what happened?" That brief flicker of a smile again. "She hauled off and hit him. Knocked out a tooth. Your grand-daddy, my father, thought it was so goddamn hilarious he offered to pay her bail straight out."

Caleb tried to reconcile the woman in the photo in his bedroom with a woman who would punch Robert Lord's father in the face. His father shook his head, the weariness returning.

"There are days when I'd love to throw both their asses in jail for a busted taillight or something stupid and let the paperwork get lost. But if I did, I'd be no better than them. You see?"

"Yessir." Caleb nodded.

He didn't see though. He knew what his father was trying to say, but some things were worth fighting for. Besides, there was no law to come in and stop Denny Harmon or Robert Lord. There was no justice unless someone like Caleb made it himself. He thought of what Cere had said on the bus: *sometimes you have to be scarier than the monsters.*

The memory of the words prickled against Caleb's skin before settling somewhere deep inside him. Maybe his father had a point. Where did it stop? He couldn't fight Robert and Denny every time they were assholes. Besides, who would the teachers, the parents, believe? Some black kid, even if he was the sheriff's son, or two nice white boys whose daddies were drinking buddies with just about everyone in town? The bag of ice on his lap spread its chill through his jeans, and Caleb set it aside.

"Between you and me?" his father said. "I hope that damned Lord boy got so scared he pissed himself."

Caleb snorted laughter, bringing a fresh spike of pain to his lip, making him cough. His father thumped him on the back.

"You know what I bet would help? Ice cream."

When Caleb got his breath back under control, his father's grin was unmistakable. At some point, Cere had slipped into the kitchen and stood in the doorway with one foot tucked behind her knee like a stork. He glanced at her, trying to tell her without words that he'd kept her secret. He couldn't guess from her expression whether she understood or if she understood the risk he'd taken. Then again, maybe that made them even, or at least closer to it.

Caleb dangled his legs over the truck's tailgate as he dug into his ice cream. He'd gotten a cup with a little plastic spoon, so he could maneuver around his split lip. Cere sat beside him, swinging her legs as she ate. Caleb watched her chase a drip of ice cream around her cone. His father was on the other side of the parking lot, talking with June and Hank Kay. Now that he and Cere were alone and there wasn't anywhere she could slip off to, questions boiled inside him again. Where had she gone when she'd snuck out of the house? What was her family really like? And most of all, what had she done to Robert?

"Your granddaddy tried to kill my granddaddy once." Cere spoke without looking at him.

"What?" Caught off guard, Caleb forgot his questions and stared at her.

"He claimed he was shooting at a deer, but my granddaddy said your granddaddy looked right at him before he pulled the trigger. When he came to see if the bullet had done the trick, my granddaddy pulled a hunting knife on him, and that's how he got away."

"I . . ." Caleb thought of the pale scar on his grandfather's hand.

He'd always assumed his grandfather had got it mending busted wire on a fence; now he tried to picture him wrestling a man with a knife. The image didn't fit, especially not the way he'd been at the end, small and hooked up to machines at Deer Creek Hospital. He had the strength of someone who'd worked a lifetime in construction, but Caleb couldn't imagine him turning that strength on anyone else unless it was in self-defense.

The night his father had found Evaneen Milton's body in the swamp—hadn't his grandfather said something about no one else having the courage to stop someone? At the time, Caleb had thought he was talking about Catfish John, but what if he meant Archie and the whole Royce family? Maybe that's why his father had been so quick to take in Cere. Maybe he felt guilty and wanted to set things right.

"I didn't know my granddaddy. My daddy told me the story, but he lied about a lot of things." Cere shrugged. Her eyes were plain hazel now, no hint of gold as she squinted in the late afternoon light.

"Your family—"

"I'm not like them." Cere cut in before he could get further.

"I didn't say you were."

Cere ignored him. "There was another story my daddy liked to tell. It was about a devil so bad even hell didn't want him. In the story, there was a preacher who made it his life's work to fight that devil. That preacher was my great, great, great, great grandpappy. And that devil was Catfish John."

Caleb sucked in a breath as Cere spoke the name he'd just been thinking.

"I don't know which parts are true, but my daddy sure believed in it, the whole thing. And it's not all lies."

Cere held out her hand, and for a moment, light gathered around it, a faint shimmer even in the bright sunlight, and then it faded.

"How do you do that?" Caleb asked.

Cere shrugged. "In my daddy's story, the preacher's son learned magic to fight the devil. He found some books no one was supposed to read, but he read them, and he passed the magic on. Most of it is learning, but what I got, it's just inside me."

Caleb thought of the gold in her eyes, the way she'd held her breath in the water and then disappeared and reappeared in the woods behind him. He thought of her shadow, unfolding and becoming larger than it should be.

"You know what I think?" A hard edge crept into Cere's voice. "I think whatever my great-great granddaddy thought he was fighting got twisted up along the line. My daddy had no idea what he was fighting, but he got so worked up about the idea of it, he didn't care if he had to burn the whole world down."

"Cere . . ."

"You want to know what I did to Robert." It wasn't a question. "I made him see."

"See what?" Caleb licked his lip, forgetting about the split and wincing when he tasted blood. The cut had opened again.

The light in Cere's eyes shifted again, the hazel swallowed in gold like someone had lifted the shade off a lantern. "What my father made me. All the things he put inside me, so I could burn the world and kill the devil."

Snake-quick, Cere clamped down on Caleb's wrist. Like a splinter forced beneath his skin, images crashed into his mind. A bloody, squalling child raised into the air. Archie Royce's face. A shout like thunder and the child dashed to the ground.

Caleb yanked his hand back. Cere let go, her expression stricken.

"I'm sorry. I didn't mean to." There was a genuine note of panic in her voice. Was that what she'd shown Robert? Cere curled her hands into her chest, hunching her shoulders. The outline of her body flickered and blurred. Just like at the creek, she was struggling with something too big to hold. "I just wanted to stop Robert and Denny from hurting you. Please don't go."

Caleb realized he'd been leaning back away from her, body tensed to flee if she reached for him again.

"It's okay." Caleb let out a shaky breath. "I'm not going anywhere."

Cere looked down, picking at an invisible scab on her knee. His head hurt as he tried to process what she'd shown him—a crying baby and Archie Royce, murdering it. The way Cere held her body made Caleb think there was more she wanted to tell him. More monsters, more terrible things just under the surface of her skin. All those years locked up in her daddy's house, had she ever had anyone to talk to? Certainly not Del. What about her other brother, Ellis?

Caleb understood loneliness, not in the same way Cere must but still. There were times the loss of his mother hurt with a sharpness that had nothing even to do with her death. No matter how much they loved him, his father and his grandparents couldn't understand what it was like living in his skin. If his mother had been alive, at least he wouldn't feel quite so alone.

At the same time, there were other things Caleb was sure he couldn't have talked to even her about. Things he didn't even want say to himself inside his own head. Like the feeling he got sometimes, watching some of the older boys at school playing basketball and baseball, or the names Robert and Denny called him. Those thoughts were too big, too dangerous.

Caleb glanced at Cere and quickly looked away. Her shoulders were still hunched, even if her outline no longer shivered. Maybe that was the way she felt all the time, like there was something huge inside her that she wanted to blurt out, but she had no idea how.

"Those names Denny and Robert called me . . ." The words started to tumble out; horrified, Caleb stopped them.

Cere stared at him, and he stared back at her until the air between them seemed to vibrate. The truth welled up in him, huge and terrifying, as big as Cere's secret. The need to tell her was almost a physical thing. She didn't know him, not really, so it would be safe. At the same time, he wanted to offer her something, like a pact made in blood or spit, because she was hurting too. But he couldn't get any farther than those first few words.

Caleb's skin felt hot. Before he could turn away, Cere reached out and touched her fingers to his split lip. It should have hurt, but it didn't.

"Shh." It wasn't a hushing gesture but a calming one.

Caleb held still, bowstring taut, but no images crashed into his mind. Cere concentrated—he could see it—letting some part of herself through but not the darkness. When Cere let her hand fall back to her lap, a faint glow lingered around her fingers. He ran his tongue over his lip. It was whole. The split was gone, and it didn't hurt anymore.

chapter four

My nana used to tell stories about songs coming out of the swamp, always on nights with heat lightning or when there was a storm waiting to break. I heard it once, only once though. I can tell you this much—whatever it was singing out there wasn't human.

I don't know if that's good or bad, but Nana knew a fellow whose bum leg got cured after hearing that song. Course, there are just as many folks who'll say the song made their daughter sick or made all their greens die. That's how it always is, the good with the bad, the miraculous with the wicked.

—*Myths, History, and Legends from the Delta to the Bayou* (Whippoorwill Press, 2016)

"Obviously Ron Butler was there, the pictures are all over the goddamn front page. What I want to know is *why*." Caleb's father held the phone receiver with one hand; the other held the *Lewis Tribune*, which he waved for emphasis as he spoke.

"What the hell happened to protecting the crime scene? Now every goddamn horse's ass who wants to see their name in print is going to come forward with 'vital information.' We might as well invite the whole goddamned town to tramp all over what little evidence we have."

Caleb's father smacked the folded newspaper against his leg before tossing it onto the kitchen counter and pinched the bridge of his nose.

"All right. I'll be there as soon as I can, and we'll work on damage control."

He hung up, and Caleb froze midway through edging toward the counter to get a look at the paper.

"Sorry. Work stuff." His father forced a smile, speaking too quickly. He tried to make it look casual as he picked up the orange juice, poured a scant inch into an already almost full glass, and put the carton deliberately on top of the newspaper.

He poured two bowls of cereal, setting them on the table, a clear indication he expected Caleb to join him. Caleb sat, but he couldn't help glancing toward the counter. His father cleared his throat, but he didn't seem to have anything to say. Caleb noted the stubble darkening his jaw.

"Are you still coming to the game tonight?" He might get a look at the newspaper if his father forgot about it. "It's just an exhibition before Summer League starts, but coach wants us all there."

"I'll do my best." His father lifted a spoonful of cereal but returned it to the bowl untouched.

Caleb forced himself not to look at the counter a second time. Had his father been talking about a new crime, or was this still about the morgue?

"Hey." The softness of his father's voice startled Caleb. Milk dripped from his spoon back into the bowl. "Look, I know I haven't been around much, but I appreciate you making Cere feel welcome."

The seriousness of his father's tone unnerved him. The way he looked at Caleb made him wonder what would happen with Cere in the future. If no other members of her family could be found, would she be shipped off to a foster home? Would she stay with them forever?

At the sound of the juice carton hitting the floor, Caleb jumped. Cere had slipped in, cat-silent as always, and she had the newspaper in her hand. Her expression was unmistakable—a shadow of the rage Caleb had seen the night her house burned.

His father moved quickly, plucking the paper from Cere's hands and crumpling it into the trash. He tried to steer Cere toward the door, but she darted past him and snatched the paper again. She tore the paper in half and in half again. Caleb could see her shaking as the pieces drifted to the ground. His father reached for her again, but she spun past him, fleeing to her room and slamming the door.

Caleb finally saw the picture on the front page. The image was grainy, showing a body beneath a tarp, one arm trailing free. He knelt, lining up the pieces to read the headline: Murder at Cult House?

His father bent to clean up the spilled juice, resigned, and Caleb turned his attention back to the paper. The wasted trees, the sparse ground—even though the burnt house wasn't visible, it had to be the woods near Archie Royce's.

Caleb looked closer. The arm was a woman's. There were marks cut into her skin, and something dark, like mud, had been packed into the wounds. His father's hand landed on his shoulder, and Caleb jumped again.

"Go see if Cere's okay."

Caleb rose and hurried from the kitchen. He knocked. No answer. Bracing himself, he tried the knob. It didn't budge. He rattled it and put his shoulder to the door. He touched the doorknob again and pulled back. It was warm, almost hot.

Caleb retreated to his own room. If Cere didn't want to talk to him, what could he do? It wasn't until he was on his way to the field for practice that it struck him: Cere's room was just like his. It didn't lock from the inside.

In the dream, Caleb followed footprints burned into the mud, the edges crisped hard like whatever had made them had baked the land dry. But even as he followed them, they shifted. Small—a heel and five toes and then wide and splayed, too-long toes joined by webs, the tips marked by the sharp point of claws.

He caught a glimpse of a woman through the trees. She looked like Cere but older. When she turned slightly, as though to make sure he was following, he could see she was heavily pregnant. When he tried to catch up, the woman walked up to the edge of the swamp as though she would walk right into the water and drown.

A massive creature rose above her, water dripping from plated scales. Caleb shouted a warning, reaching for her, and stumbled, splashing in water up to his knees. The woman vanished. There was only the monster. Too many teeth, too many mouths. It went on and on, too impossibly large to be just one thing. Other creatures or maybe parts of the same one surged around his legs—long, sinuous shapes wanting to pull him down.

Caleb shouted, thrashing and trying to kick free.

"It's okay." The voice at his ear took a moment to register.

Cere. Her arms circled him, not the muscled length of a swamp creature.

"You were having a bad dream." Her voice was calm as though there was nothing weird at all about waking to find her in his room, in his bed even. "I heard you through the wall."

She let go, and Caleb twisted around to face her. He hadn't shouted until she'd woken him; she couldn't possibly have heard him. Cere's eyes were luminous, and in the dark, he couldn't blame it on a trick of the light.

"What are you?" In the moment, Caleb didn't care how rude he sounded. She was in his room, in his bed, and he couldn't shake the fact she'd been in his dream too, crawling around inside his head. Leaving footprints in the mud. Rising out of the water.

"I am what my father made me." Cere's face, all shadow-carved, barely looked human.

"You said that before. You keep saying things that don't make any sense. Why can't you just answer me?" Caleb struggled to keep his voice low.

He held his body stiff and as far to the edge of the bed possible. The crying baby, Archie Royce's face—those weren't his memories. Those images had come from Cere.

"Just tell me what's wrong."

"I can't."

Her shadow flared; she filled every corner of the room before shrinking down to just herself again. Gold light writhed in her eyes, her lashes rimmed with tears that didn't fall.

"It's okay." Caleb took her hands. Her fingers felt like twigs. She squeezed back, hard enough to hurt.

"I don't want to . . ." Her words stuttered.

Pain arced between them as bits of darkness escaped Cere's hold. Archie Royce's hands were on him, holding him down with bruising strength. Caleb gasped, trying to pull free, but Cere held him. No, *Archie Royce* held him, speaking slick, guttural words that crawled beneath his skin.

Too big. Too much. His bones cracked. No, not his bones, Cere's. Her memories, her hurt and terror flowing through him.

A vast shape loomed over him. Them. Caleb felt himself slip even as Cere did her best to tamp down the flow of memories. But there was so much. Tendrils of solid shadow lashed the air. Things with teeth and too many eyes. Hungry things that wanted to devour the world.

A man who looked like Archie Royce—maybe the grandfather Cere had never known—summoned things from under the earth as a wide-eyed boy watched. A woman, bound to a tree, a knife pressed to her skin. Creatures born wrong, babies with no mouths or all mouth, teeth too sharp, with skin like bark, with tails. A devil with a downturned mouth, grey skin, and the blackest of eyes.

All that darkness had been shoved inside Cere, forced into her small frame. A chain of belief, warped with each generation, pulling it further out of true. *Catfish John. Catfish John.* A devil to be destroyed.

It hurt, worse than anything he'd ever felt. She'd felt. Caleb's body wanted to split at the seams, but if he let it, all that horror would be unleashed in a torrent upon the world.

"No!" Caleb jerked back, the connection broken, his hands on Cere's shoulders, pushing her away.

Cere looked as though he'd slapped her, taken her pain and shoved it back into her arms, told her she had to carry it alone. She slipped out of the bed, her eyes fixed on him, burning, but dulled by tears.

"I'm sorry. I didn't mean . . ." The hammering of his pulse calmed, coming back to normal.

Too late. She was out the door, not even bothering to close it behind her.

He heard her window slide up, rushing to his own in time to see a shadow sprint across the lawn. He couldn't let her run away again, not this upset. Caleb shoved his own window up, scrambling after her.

Branches whipped at his arms and face as he crashed into the woods bordering the property. He couldn't help picturing black lines of rot tangling his legs. The scent of char and ash, soot and damp wood, hung in the air, reaching him long before he burst out of the woods and onto Archie Royce's property. The distance cutting through the woods was less than the half mile by road, but Caleb was winded, his legs shaking as if he'd run a marathon.

He braced his hands on his knees, catching his breath. The trees that had looked sickly the night of the fire were worse now, leaning away from the remains of the house as if they could pull up their roots and flee. Between them, the skeleton of Archie Royce's house loomed. Only a small section remained intact, braced by a chimney. The rest was bones without skin.

Cere was in there somewhere.

Caleb tried to call her name, but his voice came out as a wheeze. Any moment, something monstrous would rise from the ruin, Catfish John holding Cere's remains in his claws. Rotted, scaly things crawling from under the earth and out of the swamp.

A scrabbling sound from the intact part of the house put Caleb's heart in his throat. But it was his fault Cere was here. He couldn't leave her. Without giving himself time to regret, he ducked around a blackened timber.

There was a crash, followed by a wordless yell. Caleb found Cere sitting on the floor, shoulders slumped. The room—what remained of it—held an iron bed frame, its covers and mattress burned away. Debris lay scattered all around it. Caleb found a relatively clear spot and lowered himself to the floor beside Cere. What had the room looked like before the fire? What in her father's house had she called her own?

Cere looked up. No gold threaded her eyes now. Her expression was stark despair.

"I'm sorry." It was the only thing Caleb could think to say.

Ash smeared Cere's arms, rinds of black char worked under her nails.

"There weren't enough bones."

"What?" Caleb wasn't sure if he'd misheard or just didn't understand.

"When they took my father's body away, there weren't enough bones in the ash. I kept coming back to look in case they missed something."

A knot tightened in the pit of his stomach. This is where she'd come when she'd slipped out the window the first time. How many times since? Caleb half expected the curve of ribs sticking up from under the bed or a grinning skull wedged under a fallen beam. His gaze fell on a section of wood that might once have been a closet doorframe, carved with crude notches. A prisoner, counting down days.

"I locked them in. They should have burned. But there were only remains for two people. One of my brothers is still alive."

Caleb gaped at her. She'd just admitted to locking her brothers and her father into the burning house. Had she set the fire too? Part of him might have suspected, but hearing her admit it aloud . . .

"Whichever one is alive, Ellis or Del, they stole my father's body from the morgue."

She knew about the break in and that her father's body had been stolen. What else did she know that he didn't?

"How do y—" Caleb started, but Cere cut him off.

"They murdered that woman too. The one whose picture was in the paper. Those marks cut into her skin, that's my daddy's magic. They're trying to raise the dead and bring my father back to life."

Caleb's breath caught.

"Is that . . . can they do that?"

"They were never as strong as my daddy. They weren't what he needed, but he taught Del everything he knew in case he failed, and Ellis learned from Del." Cere surprised Caleb by leaning against him, letting him take some of her weight.

"You won't tell, will you? Any of it?"

"My father could help. He's the sheriff." Caleb swallowed. The thought came back to him, the protest he'd almost made to his father about Robert and Denny and some problems being too big for the authorities. Some things you had to fight on your own.

"Would he even believe you?" Cere lifted her head.

"I . . . don't know." Caleb shrugged. His father would *want* to believe him, but how could he? On the other hand, he couldn't let Cere fight alone. All that darkness she held inside—if she unleashed it, even against her father, it would swallow her whole.

"So what do we do?"

Cere looked at him, startled. *We,* he'd said *we*. Caleb held her gaze, and didn't take the word back.

"Catfish John," Cere said after a moment. "He's not the monster everyone thinks. He helped me before. He could help me again."

Caleb thought of his grandmother's story about the girl saved from drowning. But there were more stories like the ones Robert and Denny told; he didn't know what to believe. Cere trailed her fingers through the ash, absent patterns that made Caleb's eyes hurt, so he had to look away. Cere wiped her hand on her jeans.

"People are afraid of Catfish John because of the way he looks, but real monsters don't look like monsters. They look like you and me. Especially me."

chapter five

Between 1968 and 1979, there was a string of unsolved disappearances in Sabine, Vernon, and Rapides Parishes. Seventeen women, ranging in age from sixteen to thirty-seven, went missing. Initially police assumed the women were runaways or victims of domestic violence. There was little to suggest a link between them; however, the recovery of a body in 1986, years after the last disappearance, sparked new interest in the cases.

Evaneen Milton's body was found in a swamp just outside the town of Lewis while authorities were engaged in an unrelated search for a missing girl. The remains were badly decomposed, but there was enough to show evidence of violence. When the media picked up on the story, they suggested a link between Evaneen Milton and the other missing women, and public imagination went wild. Everyone had a theory about the serial killer who was dubbed the Swamp Slasher. Though of course, other folks insisted on blaming the disappearances on Catfish John.

—*Myths, History, and Legends from the Delta to the Bayou* (Whippoorwill Press, 2016)

A MOSQUITO WHINED CLOSE TO CALEB'S EAR. HE SLAPPED IT, LEAVING A smear of blood on his palm. Between the trees, the air hung still, and on the other side of them, patches of damp opened like mouths in the ground. Light reflected in the wet, making it look like the sky come down to earth. Those patches marked the swamp's first foray into the woods surrounding them.

"Now what?" Sweat stuck Caleb's shirt to his back. They'd tramped through the woods for what felt like hours, Cere looking for just the right spot, leaving him hot and irritable.

She slung the pack she'd carried to the ground. Caleb peered over her shoulder as she drew out a cloth-wrapped bundle. His breath snagged as she unwrapped layers to reveal the wooden figurine she'd been clutching the night of the fire.

Even with the full sunlight through the trees, he couldn't make out the exact color of the wood. Dappled shadows made the carving itself seem to shift. One moment it looked like a knot of organic material, leaves and roots and flowers all wound around each other. The next, Caleb was certain it was a face, its lips thin and downturned. Then he became convinced it was actually a series of smaller, interlocking figures—fish skeletons, human bones, and deep-sea creatures making up a larger pattern. He desperately wanted to touch it, and at the same time, it disgusted him.

"What is it?" Caleb shoved his hands in his pockets.

"A song." Cere held the carving out, so the light caught the wood, making it ripple. The tangled mass seemed to uncurl, and Caleb looked away.

"Catfish John gave it to me."

Caleb glanced at her out of the corner of his eye, trying to work out how a carving could be a song. The woods had gone still, no birds, not even a mosquito since the one he'd killed.

There was another sound though, just on the edge of hearing, a faint vibration at the base of his spine. Caleb's sweat dried against his skin.

"When I was seven years old, I tried to run away from my daddy." Cere kept her eyes on the carving as she spoke, moving in a slow circle with her hands cupped in front of her.

"I didn't get far. It was rainy. I couldn't see anything, and my feet kept sticking in the mud. I wandered until I was almost in the swamp. Then I thought it would be better to drown myself than go back. That's when Catfish John found me."

She looked up. The gold in her eyes had soaked all the way through, making Caleb think of old coins. The air shivered around her hands. For a moment, Caleb could swear Cere's hands actually disappeared, taking the carving with them, so her arms ended just past her wrists. The sound at the edge of his hearing rose. Even though he could still feel the sun shining, Caleb was suddenly struck with the unshakable feeling that the sky was littered with black patches of night, impossible stars showing through.

"What—" he started, but his jaw locked.

Not just his jaw, something held his entire body still. Panic gripped him, but Cere put her finger to her lips. All Caleb could do was blink.

"I begged him to let me stay with him." Cere continued as though nothing had changed. "He said it wasn't time, but he gave me this. He said I could use it to call him. He said it would sing to me and keep me safe."

Despite the evenness of her words, Cere looked pained, Catfish John's rejection stinging even all these years later. He tried to imagine her at seven years old, wanting to drown herself rather than go back to her father. She shut her eyes, lifting the carving higher. A faint humming noise came from the back of her throat, making Caleb's scalp pull tight and the skin on his arms pucker.

He could see now that of course the carving was a song. How could he have thought otherwise? Stars glinted in the wood. Not the stars of this world, much older stars. They sang. Comforting and terrifying. Their song made him want to sleep; it made him want to scream and peel the skin from his bones.

The song continued, longer than he could bear, unwinding him, unraveling him. Then all at once, Cere's eyes flew open.

"What is it?" Cere's hold, or the song's, released Caleb, and the words tumbled out.

Cere caught his arm, digging her fingers in hard as she stared through the trees. At first, Caleb couldn't see anything. Then his eyes focused on a man the same green-grey as the patches of water between the trees.

A man, except the shape of him was wrong. Looking at him made Caleb's eyes hurt the same way the carving did. He flickered, and Caleb's gaze wanted to slide away, forget him, unsee. Beside Caleb, Cere quivered, a bow string after the arrow is loosed.

Catfish John.

The man took a shuffling step, becoming clearer and more indistinct all at once. Caleb couldn't be sure if he was actually seeing true things or if his mind filled in bits from rumors and stories. A downturned mouth, deep creases at its corners, gills slit into the side of the man's neck. Eyes, black all the way to the edges. When those eyes fixed on him, Caleb had the feeling of plunging into the creek, the water cold enough to steal his breath. Those eyes were deep as the space between stars.

All at once, the wail of a siren slammed into Caleb like a physical blow. Breath left him in a rush. He whipped around, looking for the source as it was followed by another siren and another. Through the trees, Caleb could just barely see the main road. Light skipped between the trunks as three cars from the Sheriff's department flew past.

"We have to go." Caleb grabbed Cere's arm.

She dug her heels in. He turned to find her staring at the spot Catfish John had been. They were alone.

Voices bounced through the woods, and Caleb tried to pick out his father among them. What had called the sheriff's department out here? There was nothing for miles around. Unless he and Cere had come farther than Caleb realized. He squinted. That might be the turnoff to Tupelo Campground just ahead. He let go of Cere's arm, moving closer.

One of the officers shouted, and Caleb ducked, pulling Cere with him. His pulse hammered, but the footsteps veered away. A crackle of radio static joined the jumble of voices, but Caleb couldn't make out the words. Keeping to an awkward crouch, he waddled forward, trying to get a better view.

A body lay sprawled on the leaf-strewn ground. Behind him, Caleb heard the harsh catch of Cere's breath. He twisted around to look at her. Her grim expression set a lump of cold in the pit of his stomach. This wasn't a chance hunting accident; Cere's brother, whichever one was still alive, had killed again.

He didn't have to see the body to know it would be covered with markings. Cere's expression shifted to rage. Shadows gathered and flickered around her, and the ground under them shivered. A dread certainty filled Caleb. Just like Archie Royce would tear the world apart to stop Catfish John, Cere would tear the world apart to stop her daddy.

There were no footprints in the dream this time, only a bridge jutting halfway out over a lake. At the far end, ragged chunks of concrete dropped into the water. Trees broke through the surface—a whole forest, drowned. There were dead things in the water too. Hair trailing around faces gone fish-belly pale and eyes white as polished stones. Open mouths, singing. Mark, Denny Harmon, Robert Lord. Even Caleb's father. All of Lewis was down there.

Cere stood at the far end of the bridge, only it wasn't Cere. It was the woman he'd seen in his dreams before. Light shone through her skin, and her dress fluttered against bare legs spattered with mud. She took a step toward the crumbling end of the bridge. Before Caleb could shout a warning, she let herself fall, striking the water as it boiled, a sun, ripe to bursting, unable to drown.

Caleb jolted awake. It was a moment before his room resolved around him, familiar and safe. He lay still, waiting for his pulse to slow. He couldn't shake the feeling the dreams were trying to tell him something. That they weren't just dreams but images like the ones Cere had shown him before, leaking out from her no matter how she tried to hold them in. They couldn't be memories though, so what were they? Vision of the future? Or just things that might happen? Peeling back the covers, he sat up and tapped softly on the wall separating his room from Cere's. After a moment, she tapped in return.

Light from the television shone under his father's door as Caleb crept down the hall and pushed open Cere's door. She sat with her back to him, a faint glowing surrounding her. Caleb sat beside her. She held something in her lap that looked like a bundle of rags; it was a homemade doll.

A few strands of wool clung to its scalp. Arm and leg holes had been cut into a purple Crown Royal bag, cinched at the waist with the bag's gold drawstring cord, which had been cut off and repurposed as a belt. Eyes and a mouth had been drawn on crookedly with permanent marker.

"It's not Del." Cere's eyes—green as moss, dark as mud—were threaded with dangerous light. "It's Ellis. He made this for me when I was little. I found it on the window sill."

Caleb looked from the doll to the window, imagining Cere's brother lurking in the dark, watching them.

"He didn't used to be like daddy and Del. He was different, but then . . ." Cere turned the doll over and over in her hands.

"What are we going to do?"

"Find him." Cere's grip tightened to a chokehold on the doll. "Maybe I can make him listen to me. And if I can't . . ."

Caleb saw the woman who looked like Cere, stepping off the end of the bridge and falling into the water. He saw it in Cere's eyes too. She'd rather die than let her brother use her to bring more darkness into the world.

"What happens if Ellis succeeds?"

"You've seen it already." Cere clenched her jaw.

"Not all of it. Show me the rest." He had to know why she was willing to risk her life.

Her gaze weighed on him. The nightmares were there, crawling just under the surface. It wasn't fair to let her carry it alone. Caleb reached for her hand. This time, he swore to himself he wouldn't pull away.

"Please," he said.

Cere's fingers closed on his, pale against his dark skin. Her touch plunged him into the swamp. Silt-filled water invaded his nose and mouth. Inches away, he caught sight of a muscled body like a gator's but far too big. The creature whipped around, showing a blunt mouth, eyes bulbous and wide. A fin, the impression of a gill, a claw. A face that looked terrifyingly human. Caleb kicked frantically upward, and as his head broke the surface, he drew in a stinging breath.

The world was on fire. The earth, the sky, everything. Stark against the flames stood a shadow so massive he couldn't take it all in at once. His gaze slid away, looking for something else to fix on. Ash drifted onto his face, charred bits of the sky coming away in sticky flakes. Trees grew out of the water, bodies hanging from each, bloated feet skimming the surface where vast and terrible shapes roiled.

He had to get away. Caleb panicked, batting his hands at nothing.

"Caleb!"

How long had Cere been calling his name? His cheek stung. She'd slapped him. Blood threaded from his nose. Not from her hitting him. He thought of Robert, muscles twitching as he lay in the mud beside the creek. He wiped his lip, leaving a smear of red on the back of his hand.

"We have to tell my dad about Ellis." Caleb's eyes felt too wide. Even the scant light coming under the door from the hall hurt.

"We can't."

"He can help. He's the sheriff." He'd made this argument before, and it still sounded pathetic.

"I shouldn't have showed you those things, but it's too late now. I don't want anyone else to get hurt."

Cere leaned forward, peering at him. Could she see the visions swimming in his eyes? Caleb felt them like an echo, moving beneath his skin. Was that how she felt all the time?

"Promise me?" Cere took his hand again, but this time no burning sky or tooth-filled water assaulted him.

"Okay." Caleb bit his lip.

Cere let go of his hand. He wasn't sure she believed him. He wasn't sure that she should. Shaking, he rose and padded back to his room. He'd gone to her hoping for answers, but he'd been left with more questions.

He sat in the center of his bed, pulling the covers around his shoulders and wrapping his arms around his knees. He'd promised not to say anything, but he and Cere couldn't take on her brother on their own, could they?

He thought of a night about a year ago when he and his dad had played catch out in the yard. They'd thrown the ball until it got too dark to see, and then his dad had pulled the truck around, hit the high beams, and flooded the yard, so they could keep practicing. Caleb had been nervous about making the team, but his father had said they'd practice until Caleb could throw a fastball in his sleep. Insects had swarmed the truck's lights, wings and bodies translucent as they bumped against the plastic. But they'd never gotten bit. At the time, Caleb felt like his dad had some kind of magic, holding the insects at bay.

It had been just him and his father for so long. Of course, they'd had his grandparents, but that was different. At the end of the day, it had been him and his dad against the world.

Caleb eased off the bed and peered out into the hall. Light still flickered under his father's door. Caleb glanced at Cere's door, squeezing down guilt. He was doing this to help her.

"Dad?"

He almost hoped his father wouldn't answer as he knocked softly.

"Caleb?"

The red tinge of exhaustion haunted his father's eyes as he opened his door. For a moment, he looked utterly lost, and it struck Caleb that, with his grandparents dying so close together, his father was alone now too.

"I think Cere knows something about those people who got killed." Caleb glanced over his shoulder, expecting to find Cere behind him. The hallway stood empty. "Cere thinks her brother Ellis survived the fire. She thinks he did it."

Caleb stopped, but it was too late to pretend he didn't know about the second murder. His father didn't seem to notice.

"Caleb, Ellis Royce is dead. We matched his fingerprints to what we had on file from when he and his brother broke into Hilltop."

Caleb blinked. If his father had positively identified Ellis's body, that meant . . . Del. Just like Cere had thought at first. Del must have left the doll to make her think it was Ellis.

"Then it's her other brother." Caleb's voice rose, and he fought it back down, trying to sound reasonable. "Archie Royce's body went missing, didn't it?"

Caleb licked his lips; he wasn't supposed to know about that either. The lines around his father's mouth deepened. Caleb saw the moment he came to a decision, stepping past Caleb and moving toward Cere's door. Caleb almost tried to pull him back. Instead he crowded close behind his father, ready to make his excuses to Cere. But when his father pushed open the door, the bed was empty, the sheets rumpled, the window open.

Caleb felt like an idiot. Of course, Cere had gone to deal with her brother on her own. He'd been stupid to think she'd sit around and wait. Except she still thought she was dealing with Ellis. Another thought struck him with a chill—maybe she didn't care.

"Cere's old house." Caleb moved toward the door but stopped as his father watched him in confusion.

His thoughts spun, his pulse racing. There had to be something that could help them. A sound on the edge of hearing, an itch at the base of his spine. Caleb dropped to his knees, peering under the bed.

"Caleb, what are you doing?"

He ignored his father, wiggling further into the dim space. Dust tickled his nose. The space between the bed frame and the floor was colder than it should be. Caleb stretched, concentrating on the music that wasn't music, the carving that was a song.

"Caleb, if Cere's in trouble, we have to find her."

A little further. His fingers brushed the carved wood. It squirmed under his touch. Caleb grabbed it, pretending not to feel the buzzing sensation. There was a rush of displaced air as if Caleb had taken the figurine from some space other than the one under the bed.

"Okay." Caleb scrambled to his feet before his father had a chance to ask questions. "Let's go."

Gravel crunched, red and blue lights splashing the trees as they pulled into Archie Royce's drive. His father had called for backup. Caleb watched out of the corner of his eye. What did his father think was waiting for them? A girl run away from her temporary home or something worse? His father couldn't deny the murders were real. Whether he believed they'd been committed by Cere's brother was another matter.

Caleb's father scrubbed a hand over his face and climbed out of the car, not even bothering to tell Caleb to stay behind. Caleb gripped the carved figurine, climbing out of the car as well. His father was deep in conversation with his officers; he already seemed to have forgotten Caleb's presence. Caleb took the opportunity to move toward the house.

"Cere." His voice came out as a harsh whisper, but he didn't dare raise it.

A faint glow lit the walls, charred timbers casting harsh shadows that shifted weirdly as Caleb picked his way over the broken floor. His breath echoed. It wasn't just the shadows. The house itself stretched around him. He stumbled, going to one knee.

He pushed himself up, rubbing ash from his palms. It clung to him like the black rot on the lawn. That seemed like a lifetime ago. Distracted, Caleb didn't notice the figure until it grabbed his arm, and he let out a yell. A face leered close, eyes full of sick, burning light, mouth a slit in a black, tangled beard. Del.

Caleb tried to back away, but his feet slipped on the floor. Del smelled of rot mingled with sweat.

"Help!" Caleb found his voice, hoping his father would hear.

"Shut up."

With his free hand, Del smacked Caleb—hard enough his head rocked to the side, leaving his ears ringing—and dragged him deeper into the house.

Shouts sounded behind them; two flashlight beams cut through the dark. Shadows jumped, and Caleb was momentarily blinded. He raised his hand to shade his eyes as one of his father's officers appeared in the doorway, Caleb's father behind him.

"Caleb!"

Caleb's chest tightened. He'd put them all in danger, and he hadn't even managed to help Cere.

"Let go of the boy and put your hands where we can see them."

An officer Caleb didn't recognize spoke as his father took a step forward. Del pulled Caleb closer, the scent of him making Caleb's eyes water.

Del snarled, spitting a word old and ugly and not in any language Caleb knew. It flew through the air, a solid clot of darkness—thick and tarry—striking the officer and knocking him flat, his flashlight spinning away.

"Stop." Cere's voice rang through the house.

A shadow separated from the wall, becoming a girl. For a moment, she had too many angles. Bones seemed to jut from her shoulders, clattering like terrible wings. Then she was just Cere, her chin up, her eyes—which were every color and no color—swarming with gold.

Even Del froze although his grip remained tight on Caleb's arm.

"Del."

"Heya, sissy." The words dripped malice, but even so, Caleb felt Del tense. He was afraid of Cere.

"Let Caleb go." Cere's voice was low.

"Caleb. Oooh, Caleb." Del crooned, making Caleb's name sound like an ugly thing. It made him think of Denny and Robert. He shook Caleb, making his already aching head rattle. "This little nigger your boyfriend?"

Cere didn't react. She stared at Del, and Caleb felt the air around him crackle. Tendrils of shadow unfolded behind her and one of those shadows lashed the air next to Del's head, cracking like a whip. Del jerked to the side, shoving Caleb away from him. A smell like ozone lingered in the air.

Caleb climbed to his feet and froze. Everything froze. It was like it had been in the woods when they'd gone searching for Catfish John. He could see and hear everything, but he couldn't turn his head, couldn't speak. His father and the other officers seemed frozen too. Only Cere moved, approaching her brother.

"This is between kin, Del."

"Just right, little sister. A happy family reunion like daddy would've wanted." Del grinned, showing crooked teeth.

The house expanded, the angles of it gone wrong. The burned walls rolled back, revealing an ashen plane dissected by fallen beams. The house was still there, but the pieces of it didn't match up. It reminded Caleb of a card game he used to play with his grandparents where each card was a piece of the house the players had to assemble.

Overhead, scraps of sky had been torn away, showing stars that had no business here. They made Caleb think of eyes, opening and blinking in the dark.

Caleb still had Catfish John's carved figure shoved into the pocket of the cargo shorts he'd hastily pulled on before they left the house, but he couldn't reach it, not with his hands stuck at his sides. But he could still hear it. He strained to catch the weird melody over the thump of blood in his ears while Del and Cere circled each other, wary animals. Cere had said Catfish John had given it to her to call him if she needed him. Caleb couldn't think of a better time, but would it work for him?

Catfish John.

Caleb let them name roll through his head like a bell. He didn't know how it was supposed to work, but what else could he do?

"Let them go." Cere kept her eyes on Del.

"Or what?" Del's tone mocked. His tangled beard and matted hair made him look ancient, but somehow Cere seemed like the elder sibling.

"I know what I was made for." Cere stepped closer, scarcely coming to the middle of Del's chest, but he flinched. "Do you?"

Del puffed himself up, but his voice shook.

"You are a tool to do our father's work."

Caleb tried to look toward his own father, but the angle was wrong. A shiver ran through the house, charred wood and stone grinding against each other. The leaf-rot and silt scent of the swamp rose around them. Water sloshed in the dark, but Caleb couldn't see it.

"You're nothing without Archie." Cere's tone turned as nasty as Del's.

Del leapt for her, but Cere jumped back. Shadows engulfed her for a moment, and she reappeared on the other side of him, shaking. Caleb could see the effort it cost her; she was doing her best to hide it, but she was scared. The light in Del's eyes shifted, a tint of red joining the muddy light like blood spreading through water.

A hum, a vibration deep in Caleb's bones. A different kind of song, one that called things out of the earth, out of the grave. It came from Del. Caleb realized his concentration had slipped. He couldn't hear Catfish John's song anymore.

Catfish John.

He thought the name frantically now, reaching after the threads of unearthly music.

Del's song was louder, a horrid wet sound that wasn't music at all. It was a hand, pressing Caleb down. His legs buckled, slamming him to his knees. The pressure continued. If it didn't let up, he would shatter.

A glow gathered around Cere's skin. She breathed hard, her eyes wide. From here, instead of mossy grey-green or even gold, they appeared black as polished stone. Caleb clung to Catfish John's name, repeating it in his mind, trying to block out Del and everything else. He tried to remember the way he'd felt in the woods when Cere held the carving in her hands. A lullaby in a tangle of wood, the light of strange stars, cool water to wash away the muck Del called.

Something rotting crawled past Caleb, something that looked like an animal turned inside out. He thought of Del on the train tracks. He imagined Del, torturing animals and burying them all over Archie Royce's property. The dead thing slithered past, followed by another and another.

Caleb look away, focusing on Cere instead. A faint tremor ran beneath her skin. Del's song pulled at her, trying to break the dam and set the darkness free. Even Caleb could feel it, sluggishly rooting around the edges of his mind.

Cere clenched her fingers, answering Del with a note of her own—high, piping, and strange. Was this the magic Archie taught, or was this something else? Slick shapes writhed in the air. Caleb's upper lip tickled. Blood threaded from his nose, but this time he couldn't wipe it away. It fell in fat, crimson drops to the ash-strewn ground.

"Give up." Cere spoke between gritted teeth. "Archie is dead. You don't have to do what he says anymore."

Del let out a roar, an almost human sound in contrast to the weird of his song. His hand flashed out, catching Cere's cheek. She spun with the blow, losing her balance and hitting the ground. Her song cut off.

Caleb gagged, a taste like wet and rotting leaves clotting his tongue. Catfish John. He tried again to focus on the name. Cere climbed to her feet. Had she made Del angry on purpose to distract him?

Caleb's fingers twitched. His muscles ached. If he could reach the carving . . .

Cere lashed out not with shadows but her own fingers, hooked like claws and tearing at Del's skin. Her narrow chest heaved. Even if she was trying to distract Del, her own concentration was spread thin. How long could she fight him off, hold herself together, and keep everyone still and safe out of the way? Her body was still human even if she'd been born to channel Archie's private apocalypse. Eventually she would wear down.

Catfish John. Caleb focused on his breath, his pulse, let the name match their rhythm. His fingers twitched again. He almost shouted with relief. Another twitch. A sliver of motion.

Cere's breath came in shallow gasps, but at least, Del seemed to be tiring too. The air around them crackled and burned, and Caleb caught glimpses of the things he'd seen in Cere's nightmares. The torn patches in the sky showed blood red now. Cere flickered, becoming the pregnant woman from Caleb's dreams and then something else entirely. A vast, scaled creature, the crown of her head scraping the broken sky.

Caleb squeezed his eyes shut, feeling a rush of victory when he realized he could. He closed the distance to his pocket and yanked out the wooden figure. Its curves felt warm and smooth beneath his touch.

"Please." He fought the word past his lips. "Help her."

He opened his eyes, clenched his jaw. Light bled from Cere's skin, making it look almost translucent. Shadows moved beneath its surface like terrible bruises. She shuddered, curling inward like she could hold onto everything by making herself small. Del grinned, his face horribly lit with triumph. The ground heaved. One of the remaining sections of wall cracked, showering them with brick dust.

"Please," Caleb whispered, hoarse. "Catfish John."

All at once, the pressure lessened. Caleb sucked in a breath. Cere had resumed her song, and now a third voice threaded between Cere's and Del's, between the dark shapes crowding the air. It wasn't anything human, yet it was comforting. Safe. To Caleb, it sounded like his mother's barely remembered singing, tasted like his grandmother's persimmon jelly, felt like sunshine on his shoulders as he and Mark lazed by the creek. It was his grandfather's stories and playing catch with his father.

Cere froze, crouched and looking up at her brother. Del froze too. Caleb realized he could turn his head now.

Catfish John. Here, actually here. He'd answered Caleb's call.

Catfish John's music rose, steady and rolling as he approached Archie Royce's children. Cere straightened and took a limping step, her posture speaking pain and longing. Her skin cracked, bits of her flaking away to ash. Everything she was holding inside wanted to come out and devour the world even when Del's song fell still.

Caleb could almost see Catfish John clearly, but even this close, something about him seemed to resist the eye. Grey skin, the downturn of his mouth. He wore an old hunting jacket, collar turned up, but it couldn't quite hide the slits in his neck. Gills. Or maybe just scars, marks of violence done against him for being different. Catfish John was both and neither—a man who just wanted to be left alone, a being older than the world.

The two images resolved in Caleb's mind, collapsing into one. It didn't matter what Catfish John was: Cere believed in him, so Caleb would too.

Del's eyes widened as Catfish John stopped in front of him.

"You." The word stuttered.

The blood-red tint left Del's eyes, going muddy dark. What stories had Archie told him about the creature in front of him, the devil so bad even hell didn't want him? Caleb surprised himself with a moment of pity for Del. The man who tortured animals, who'd tried to hurt Cere, looked small, lost. Catfish John towered over him, at least nine feet tall and growing. The teeth in that downturned mouth were wicked sharp; those webbed hands could so easily snap Del's neck.

Two devils, one human and one not, a holy man and a wanderer from outside the world, battling down through time.

Del's mouth stretched in an expression of horror. Caleb struggled to keep his eyes on what was happening, but it blurred. He was underwater. He was drifting off to sleep. His grandmother, mother, father, singing him a lullaby.

Caleb yawned so wide his jaw cracked. Del swayed on his feet. Catfish John reached out and touched Del's forehead. Or Caleb thought he did. Space folded and the stars rushed backward. Del howled, a feral sound of rage like the sound that had come over the trees the night Evaneen Milton's bones were found. The sound the face in the smoke had made the night Archie Royce's house burned. The sound of loss Cere made when Catfish John left her behind.

They blended in Caleb's head. Del dropped, a boneless sack of clay. Catfish John's hand hung in the air for a moment, his webbed fingers glimmering. His shoulders stooped, shorter than Caleb's father. How had Caleb ever thought he was nine feet tall?

"Child." Catfish John's voice echoed; Caleb felt it in his bones more than heard it.

The word might have been for Cere, or it might have been for Del. Or maybe Catfish John hadn't spoken at all.

Cere wrapped her arms around her body. She shook but not with sobs. Bits of her skin peeled away, mouths opening to show the darkness within. Catfish John held out a hand to her.

All the while, his song continued. Singing Cere down, singing her back into herself.

Cere took his hand. The ground stopped shuddering. Catfish John turned toward the woods, leading Cere at his side.

"No." The shout broke from Caleb. He took a step, his entire body aching. "Where are you taking her?"

"Caleb." Caleb's father, unfreezing, caught Caleb's shoulder.

Caleb turned. His father looked bloodless in the dark, worn out and terrified. A burst of static as one of the other officers pulled out a radio and called for more backup. The world poured back in all at once.

Catfish John stopped, and Caleb caught his breath. An ancient thing, a wounded man. The dark of Catfish John's eyes went all the way to the edges. They made Caleb think of the night sky, speckled with stars. Sorrow, older than he could imagine, and weariness as well.

Caleb's father tightened his grip on Caleb's shoulder, his hand shaking.

"It's okay." Cere's voice was rough with strain.

She looked up at Catfish John and slipped her hand from his webbed one. She came toward Caleb and his father. She hugged them each in turn. Heat from her skin soaked through Caleb's clothes. He could feel her bones and, sliding just under the surface, the nightmares she held at bay.

Threads of darkness writhed in Cere's eyes—black against gold. They were the things from under the water, the creature Caleb had seen her become, the thing whose head scraped the sky.

"It'll be okay," she said. "I promise."

She turned back to Catfish John, taking in his hand again. She looked over her shoulder, meeting Caleb's eyes.

"Thank you." She smiled, and for once, it wasn't shadowed with pain. For this moment at least, when Cere burned, it was pure light.

"Wait!" Caleb held out the carving. He had almost forgotten it, but when he uncurled his fingers, the strange lines of it were pressed into his palm.

"This is yours." He handed it to Cere; a shock like an electric spark jumped between them.

Catfish John's attention shifted, fixing on Caleb. He felt seen, picked apart and known. All of his secrets, all of his fears—Robert Lord and Denny Harmon—they were small enough for Catfish John to hold in his hand. He imagined them, stardust in that strange, webbed palm, blown away in a simple puff of breath. Catfish John inclined his head, almost a nod. Caleb felt a weight lifted off his chest, but he was too dazed to speak.

Then Catfish John turned, leading Cere with him. The moon was still up, the stars—the real ones—still bright, but the sky glowed like the rising sun. A crack in the world. It silhouetted them as they walked side by side—the not-quite-human figure of Catfish John and Cere, looking small and fragile.

Caleb watched, his eyes burning, until the light went out. The wail of a siren cut through the night. The sky returned to its usual blue-black, slightly hazy, and the house was just a house, not an impossible, ruined labyrinth.

"She'll be okay." His father's voice was quiet.

Caleb wanted to believe him. And he wanted to argue; they needed to bring Cere home. His father gave Caleb's shoulder a squeeze before going to meet the ambulance.

Lights flashed. Voices swirled around him. Inertia kept Caleb where he was, watching the world happen around him. It was an effort to stay upright, keep his eyes open. Each blink seemed to last longer than the one before. At some point, he noticed Del no longer lay crumpled on the ground. Had the ambulance taken him?

Caleb picked his way back to the driveway and sat with his back against the reassuring solidity of his father's car. He watched the sun come up, true dawn. When his head got too heavy, he lay down, curling on his side. Later he was vaguely aware of someone lifting him into the car.

In half-dreams, things swarmed around him in the water. Cere, bright and round as the sun, stood on the edge of a bridge and held out her hand.

The sound of the car door opening woke him. Caleb sat up as his father climbed into the front seat, sitting with his hands on the wheel. His shoulders sagged; his face in the rearview mirror had aged five years.

With a sigh, he started the car, executing a turn back toward the road.

"What about Cere?" Caleb's voice felt thick as if the brutal force of Del's magic or Catfish John's calming song still clung to him.

His father tapped the brake as if caught by surprise. The car stuttered before continuing to roll.

"We'll find her."

In the rearview mirror, his father's gaze slid away. He frowned like he was trying to remember something. As Caleb watched, the lines in his face smoothed into blank exhaustion. Caleb twisted around to look at the remains of Archie Royce's house.

"We can't just leave her."

His father startled again, opening his mouth as if to shape the word *who.*

The lines around his mouth deepened as he closed it, but he didn't stop the car.

A faint sense of panic tapped against Caleb's ribs. Cere. Catfish John. It had happened. He tried to hold onto the image of them walking away, but it clouded at the edges.

"Hmm?" His father, distracted, glanced in the rearview mirror.

Cere's name stuck on Caleb's tongue, refusing to shape itself aloud. Was that Catfish John's last gift to her, a way to protect her?

What had his father seen when Del and Cere faced each other? Had he heard the lullaby? Caleb shook his head like he was trying to dislodge water in his ear.

His father pulled onto the main road. Caleb could barely keep his eyes open. His chin dipped toward his chest. He jerked back, pulse skittering.

He had to stay awake. He had to help Cere.

The thought twisted away from him. Cere was somewhere else. She was safe.

No. Someone had taken her. She was in danger.

The thoughts jumbled; he couldn't pick the threads apart. This time when his head nodded, he didn't fight it. He let sleep pull him down, away from nightmare visions of the burning sky and the water full of teeth. Even though they were already pulling back into his grandparents' driveway, Caleb let himself drift away.

His last conscious thought was of the strange melody of a lullaby.

part 3

2014

chapter one

The stories about Catfish John range all over the place, just like the names for him. He's a genetic experiment gone wrong, something cooked up by the government to fight the Ruskies. He's an escaped circus freak. A patient from an insane asylum. He's a man who just wants to be left alone. He's a devil, cursed by God to wander the earth forever, looking for forgiveness. Some folks honestly believe a human woman and an alligator got together and birthed a creature in-between, a monster.

—*Myths, History, and Legends from the Delta to the Bayou* (Whippoorwill Press, 2016)

Caleb followed the footprints sunk deep into the mud, just like he had when he was twelve years old. He passed the ruins of a house that no longer existed and went into the swamp as the sun was rising. Flat pools of water gathered around cypress knees caught the light, gleaming like liquid fire. A line of gold at the horizon spread, not the sun but a crack in the sky. A shadow emerged, and the mud around Caleb's feet bubbled as something rose.

Gold eyes. Scales, rough as the bark of an ancient tree. A gator bigger than any he'd ever seen, standing on its hind legs like something human, cradling its heavy belly in clawed limbs.

"It's time," it said in Cere's voice, mouth doubled and trebled, speaking as a child, a woman, a thing with too many teeth.

"It's time." Kyle nudged him.

The shrill of a strange swamp bird became the alarm on Caleb's phone.

"I'm awake." He fumbled to swipe the alarm off and let his arm fall across his eyes.

"You could call in sick." Kyle poked him in the side; Caleb squirmed away.

"Can't." Caleb didn't lift his arm. "Wouldn't do for Lewis's youngest-ever sheriff to start slacking off less than a year into the job."

He forced himself to sit up, squinting.

"Not to mention its first queer sheriff." Kyle poked him in the side again.

"Wait'll they find out I'm black too." He untangled his legs from the sheet and stood.

"I'll never tell." Kyle put both hands over his mouth and then lowered them with a grin.

"How *did* you get elected?" Kyle reached for the jeans crumpled on the floor.

"I told them I was a Republican." Now it was Caleb's turn to grin.

Kyle grabbed a towel slung over the end of the bed and tossed it at Caleb's head.

"Blasphemy."

Caleb caught the towel but felt his grin slip, a nerve struck.

"Honestly I'm afraid I'm just trading on my father's reputation, and it's only a matter of time before someone comes to tell me it was all a mistake and kicks me out of office."

"Hey." Kyle's voice softened, and Caleb looked up. "You're a good sheriff. You've done a lot for this town in just a few months."

"I guess." Caleb slung the towel over his shoulder, trying to put his smile back in place, even if he didn't feel it. Kyle didn't look convinced.

Caleb couldn't help his doubts. Even if he single-handedly saved the whole town from burning down, he'd never live up to his father's reputation. Of course, with most of Lewis's offenses being traffic tickets, petty vandalism, and one property line dispute between neighbors that had come to blows, Caleb wasn't exactly saving the world, which didn't help his confidence either.

He ducked into the shower, letting needles of hot water scrub away the green rot of his dream, trying to send the feelings of self-doubt with it. Both lingered. Even standing on the shower's slick tile, Caleb felt mud squelch between his toes. The dreams had been getting worse lately, more frequent, and from the way Kyle looked at him some mornings, Caleb knew he wasn't hiding it particularly well. That worried look, the one he caught Kyle at when he thought Caleb wasn't looking, came more and more frequently these days too.

When they'd first met, Kyle had just moved from Kansas after dropping out—burning out, he'd said—of grad school, working odd jobs while he tried to figure out his life. He'd been studying comparative religion and mythology with the idea of eventually going into teaching, but after what he'd described as a series of low-level panic attacks, he'd decided to hide himself in a town where no one knew him.

Their actual meeting had been almost a rom-com meet cute, at least a rom-com meet cute for rednecks. Without thinking, Kyle had cheered a Chiefs touchdown against the Saints in Woody's Bar amidst a sea of black and gold jerseys, and Caleb had swooped in like a knight in shining armor and saved Kyle from getting his ass beat. Of course, on their second date, Caleb had made Kyle swear up and down that he would never cheer for any team playing against the Saints in Caleb's hearing ever again. That had been almost three years ago, before he was even Sheriff, and Caleb was still amazed Kyle had stayed instead of leaving Lewis in his rearview mirror.

He was even more amazed Kyle had stayed after the first time Caleb had woken up screaming from a nightmare. But he had, and he'd been infinitely patient, even helping Caleb chase down legends about Catfish John. That crease of worry between his eyes never quite went away though. Caleb suspected part of Kyle's willingness to help stemmed from a hope that somehow, if they could find a real historical basis for Catfish John, the obsession would go away. The nightmares would stop. Caleb would be "normal" again.

Caleb scrubbed his hands over his face, shutting off the water. He stood dripping, letting his skin cool. He'd tried to explain to Kyle how the dreams felt realer than real, how he wasn't even sure they were dreams, how they might be visions, and how he couldn't shake the certainty Cere was out there somewhere. Still alive. And it was only a matter of time before she came home.

He stepped out of the shower and toweled himself dry. The image of his father, lying in the hospital bed and looking so much like Caleb's grandfather had at the end, rose sharp in his mind. Maybe Caleb should have tried to talk to him about the night Cere disappeared one more time before the end. But it had seemed pointless. His father could barely remember Cere by the time they'd pulled out of Archie Royce's driveway. What would be the use of dragging up her name when his father was hooked up to machines, the x-rays of his lungs an eerie echo of Caleb's grandmother's and grandfather's before him.

The few times over the years Caleb had tried bringing up Cere only got him further from the truth. His father might vaguely recall a few details if Caleb prompted him, but Caleb could never tell whether those were true memories or his own suggestions working their way into his father's mind. It was eerie. His father had an almost photographic memory for cases years old; he could still recite word for word books like *The Lorax*, which he'd read to Caleb as a kid. But with Cere, it was like something had taken her completely out of his father's memory.

When it came right down to it, Caleb could barely trust his own memories. If he left them alone too long, they changed. Had it been Del or Ellis in the house that night? Was Catfish John's skin grey or green?

That was the other thing he couldn't quite explain to Kyle—if he didn't keep obsessively telling himself the story of Cere, searching for fragments of Catfish John's story to back his memories up, then he would lose her completely. It would be as though she'd never existed at all. The rest of Lewis had moved on, the wound scabbing over. Even the remains of Archie Royce's house had been razed. Now only an empty lot stood where it had once been.

Caleb swiped condensation from the mirror and picked up his razor. No matter how the land changed, no matter the worry in Kyle's eyes or the dreams that plagued him, he wouldn't let Cere vanish a second time.

"Morning, boss. Coffee." Rose Jackson, Caleb's chief deputy, handed him a travel mug as he climbed out of the car.

"I can't help noticing it's to go." Caleb frowned as Rose steered him back toward the car.

"That's the bad news. Call came in while you were on your way. I figured I'd give you ten minutes grace and wait until you got here. A body was found out by Emmett Hawkins's place. Emmett's out of town visiting his great-granddaughter. The kids he was paying to keep an eye on his house found the corpse."

"That's the bad news. What's the good news?"

"You have coffee." Rose gave him a wry grin.

Caleb sighed and started the car as Rose climbed in beside him. He pulled out of the lot, flipping on the siren as he did. Despite Rose's words, her expression was grim, her humor armor against the less savory aspects of their job. In their time together, Caleb had had the opportunity to see many versions of Rose's armor, and each one made him like her more.

A month after he'd appointed her, they'd been at the Hilltop, picking up sweet tea, and had chanced to overhear Nathan Hawley grumbling to Sheila Hannerity at the register about the "type" taking over law enforcement in Lewis. Obviously Nathan hadn't seen either of them, but Rose had stepped right over to Nathan, wearing a smile sharp enough to draw blood. She'd stuck out her hand to shake, standing in a way that made her height advantage over him clear, and in a honeyed drawl nothing like her normal speaking voice, she'd said, "I surely hope I can live up to the reputation that must have preceded me in order for you to be putting me in a class with our fine sheriff here."

Caleb had nearly choked on suppressed laughter, watching Nathan and Sheila turn the color of sour milk, looking twice as curdled. It wasn't until they were both back in the car that Rose allowed her hands a faint tremor, and Caleb had reassured her Nathan's bark was worse than his bite.

"So I won't be waking up to any burning crosses on my lawn?" Rose had quirked an eyebrow, even though her expression had remained shaky.

"Nah. That'd require him to be able to operate lighter fluid and a match without setting himself ablaze, and he's a little gun-shy since he blew his eyebrows off at a cookout last Fourth of July."

Rose snorted, and Caleb had been relieved to see her relax, realizing just how sorry he'd be to lose her. He had, however, proceeded to give her a rundown of who she did need to keep an eye out for, including Robert Lord's sorry excuse for a father, who continued to cling to Lewis even though Robert and the rest of the family had long since moved on.

Despite the scene they were driving to now, Rose seemed as steady as ever, and Caleb found himself grateful all over again. She'd grown up somewhere near Tallahassee, and for the life of him, he couldn't figure out what she wanted with a small nowhere town like Lewis. Her claim was that she'd thrown a dart at a map and ended up with Lewis, but he didn't believe her. For one thing, who even kept paper maps anymore?

Yellow safety tape fluttered around the shallow ditch beside Emmett Hawkins's drive as Caleb pulled off to the side of the road.

"Brief me?" Caleb took a sip of his coffee, making a face at the bitter-burnt flavor, and abandoned the mug in the cup holder.

"Not much." Rose nodded toward two other officers. "They're just getting started. The report is pretty fresh."

Caleb approached, thumbs tucked into his belt. It was an affectation he'd picked up from television, and it annoyed him every time he caught himself doing it. He put his hands behind his back instead.

"Anything yet?"

Terry Rowe, a man who'd joined the department under Caleb's father, looked up.

"Blunt force trauma to the head. Not much blood. Looks like she was killed elsewhere and dumped here." Terry paused, a frown working the corners of his mouth.

"And?" Caleb braced himself; there was something Terry wasn't saying.

"Maybe you'd better see for yourself."

Terry's frown further soured the coffee in Caleb's stomach. Terry peeled back the covering over the body, and the world jolted out of time. Markings covered the dead woman's arms, wounds packed with black mud to make them stand out. For a moment, Caleb was twelve, looking at a grainy newspaper photograph.

He's trying to bring my father back. Cere's voice in his head and again in his dream, *It's time.*

Caleb shook himself, forcing his attention back to the present. It had to be a copycat killer. But two victims wasn't exactly the kind of murder spree that inspired imitators. Besides, most people in Lewis didn't even remember the murders—or anything else connected to the Royce family—unless Caleb outright reminded them. Or unless evidence was staring them in the face.

"Just like last time." Terry echoed Caleb's thoughts, but there was an edge of uncertainty as if he wasn't quite sure what he meant.

"Aw, shit!"

"Deputy?" Rose's exclamation drew Caleb's attention.

"I know her." Rose crouched by the body. "That's Holly DuBois. We went to college together. We were paired up as roommates for a semester before she dropped out."

"You're sure?" Caleb was annoyed with himself the moment he said it, but the look Rose gave him was troubled rather than angry.

"Yeah."

Only then did Caleb think to touch her shoulder, a comforting hand. Rose took a deep breath and straightened.

How would his father have handled the situation? Better certainly.

"If you'd rather sit this one out . . ." Caleb started, but this time, the look Rose turned on him was unmistakably a glare. He held up his hands. "Okay sorry."

"What did Rowe mean by 'just like last time'? Sounds like something out of a damned horror movie." Rose had regained her composure although her gaze kept sliding back to Holly.

Caleb glanced at Terry who stood a few paces off, talking to the coroner who had just arrived.

"Come over for a drink after work. I'll catch you up, and you can tell me about Holly DuBois."

Rose shot him a questioning look, but Caleb only shrugged. Maybe he was paranoid, but he wasn't convinced one of the other officers wouldn't use anything they might overhear to discredit him. Besides, he needed the time to get his thoughts in order.

"Fresh from the icebox and fresh from the yard." Kyle handed Caleb and Rose each a beer, followed by a dish of sliced peaches topped with vanilla ice cream.

"Beer and dessert." Rose grinned. "This one's a keeper."

"Don't I know it," Caleb said as Kyle took the third porch chair, splaying out his long legs.

"My grandmother's not-so-secret cure-all. Though she preferred bourbon to beer." Kyle raised his bottle, and Rose clinked hers against it.

Caleb couldn't help flashing back to when he'd first introduced them. Even though his sexuality wasn't exactly a secret around the office, Rose was the first and only person he'd felt comfortable "flaunting" it around as it were. Kyle and Rose had taken an instant liking to each other, and Caleb had only regretted the introduction in so far as they had spent most of the night trying to outdo each other with embarrassing stories about him.

"Do you know I had to teach him how to line dance?" Kyle had said, grinning from ear to ear. "What kind of self-respecting Southern boy doesn't at least know how to boot scoot?"

Caleb had tried to protest he wasn't that kind of cowboy, and Rose had launched into a story about how scandalized Caleb had been the time they'd been called in on a report of trespassing to find Cole Richards with his pants around his ankles and his bare ass stuck in a feed bucket in Pete Lawton's barn. He'd been high as a kite and claimed he'd just been looking for a place to piss, but with Pete's heifers lowing and rolling their eyes, the inevitable jokes had started, and Rose had barely been able to keep it together while Caleb looked like he'd wanted to crawl into a hole and die.

Caleb caught himself grinning like an idiot at the memory and wiped the smile away, turning his attention to the dessert. The peaches had been warming all day in the sun, and they still held a hint of that warmth. The sudden image of a persimmon from his grandmother's tree, oozing black rot, stole his fleeting good mood. He inspected the peaches, swallowing hard, and forced himself to take a bite to prove he could before pushing the bowl away.

"Catch me up, boss." Rose nudged the toe of Caleb's boot.

Caleb passed a hand over his hair. Rose deserved the truth inasmuch as he could give it.

"When I was a kid . . ."

"This is about Cere." Kyle sat up, tension lifting his shoulders.

Caleb spread his hands, shrugging. Even if he had wanted to let it go, he couldn't anymore. A woman had died. Someone Rose knew. Kyle sat back, but the expression of worry didn't leave his face.

Since the third month of their relationship, when they'd stopped simply meeting up and started staying over, Kyle had been privy to the worst of Caleb's nightmares. Those times Caleb woke shouting Cere's name, flailing and knocking over lamps. He had every right to worry.

Caleb knotted his fingers, looking down but feeling Rose's attention as he related the story.

"I know how it sounds," he said when he'd run out of words. "There are times when even I think I imagined the whole thing."

It was only the second time he'd told the story in full, and it left him as wrung-out as the first.

"I've heard of Catfish John." Rose tapped at her beer bottle thoughtfully. "My uncle had stories about him, called him the River Man, but they sound pretty much the same." She shrugged, killing the rest of her beer. She set her bottle down. "Del Royce did murder two people. That's a fact. It's in your father's files. So wouldn't all the rest be in there too?"

"Some. Not all."

With everything his father had done for Lewis, had done for Cere before she disappeared, Caleb didn't want this one failure to be the thing that defined him. Rose had never met his father, Kyle either. It wasn't the image he wanted to give them, but how else could he explain things?

"It's . . . the case is still open, unsolved. My father didn't stop looking, but . . . every time I tried to ask him, he would get this far-away look, like he couldn't remember. Like something kept him from remembering." Caleb spread his hands again, a helpless gesture.

Following Rose's example, Caleb took the last swallow of his beer and gave Rose a half smile.

"Thinking about a career change yet?"

"I've heard wilder things. Seen 'em too. You never met my granny." Rose flashed a wicked grin.

"Oh?" Caleb raised an eyebrow, the knot in his chest loosening. "You'll have to tell me your war stories someday, but for now, tell me about Holly?"

"Hmm." Rose pulled out her phone, scrolling as she talked. "Like I said, she dropped out our first semester. Had this older guy she was involved with. I think she thought he was going to pay her way or something."

She held her phone out to Caleb.

"Just a week ago, Holly posted something for Throwback Thursday on Facebook and tagged me. We weren't friends, but you know how it is."

"Woah. You had a full-on Pam Grier, didn't you?" Caleb ran a hand over his own close-cropped hair again.

Rose was the one black face in a group of white kids. He thought back to Mark, their little band of two. At least college had been better for him, but it didn't look like it for Rose.

He knew it hadn't been easy for Mark either. Even though they'd gone to separate colleges, they'd kept in touch. About a month or two after 9/11, the sandwich shop Mark's parents ran in Lewis was vandalized, the windows smashed in, slurs spray-painted on the walls. It didn't matter that they weren't Muslim; they were brown, and that was enough for some of the good old boys. Caleb's father's health had already been failing then, and he'd turned over the lead in the investigation to other members of the department. Shortly after their shop was vandalized, the Nayar's house was broken into. They'd decided that was enough and moved away.

Caleb hadn't seen Mark since the first summer back from college. They exchanged emails on their respective birthdays, but that was it. He'd never asked Mark if he remembered Cere or the day they'd seen Del Royce torturing an animal on the train tracks. He was afraid of what the answer might be.

"Retro was cool back then." Rose gave him a sour look, bringing Caleb back to the present. Her hair now was practically as short as his. "Anyway, that's Holly."

She pointed, and Caleb enlarged the image, trying to match the girl in the picture to the dead woman in the ditch. Even without the marks cut into her skin, Holly had looked like someone used hard by life. The girl in the picture at least looked like she had some hope.

Rose leaned over, scrolling the image a bit to the left.

"That's the guy she was seeing. The one she dropped out of college for."

Caleb nearly dropped the phone. He'd been so focused on Holly he hadn't looked closely.

"That's Del."

The rotten-sour stench of him, his hot breath against Caleb's cheek as he'd snarled a word into the air and taken down one of his father's men. Tim Vickers had been in and out of hospitals and doctors' offices with health problems the rest of his life, ones he'd never had before. Toward the end, lesions in his throat and on the lining of his stomach had made it so he could barely eat. He'd starved to death.

Poison. Tim Vickers. Caleb's grandmother, his grandfather, even his father. As much as he hated it, Caleb religiously went to the doctor every year for a full checkup. So far, he had a clean bill of health, but what if the rot that had taken the rest of his family was just waiting for him? Maybe he'd gotten lucky, maybe he hadn't lived in his grandparents' old house long enough. But what if he was a carrier somehow? What about Kyle?

He pushed the thought away, enlarging the picture again. Sunken cheeks, shaggy hair, eyes that had once turned red like blood in water. Had Del spent all this time hidden in plain sight, looking for Cere? How had Caleb missed him? Caleb imagined Del separating Holly from her peers, encouraging her to drop out, turning her into someone who would never be missed. Keeping her around until he needed her.

"You think this is the guy who killed her? The same one who killed those two people when your father was sheriff?" Rose took the phone back.

"At least two." Caleb shook his head. "I never saw what happened to Del the night Cere vanished. Catfish John did something to him and then . . ." Caleb shrugged.

"Or there's a copycat killer on the loose." Kyle echoed Caleb's earlier thoughts.

They lapsed into silence, and Kyle stood.

"I think we need another round."

"So what do we do?" Rose asked as Kyle returned with fresh beer. "How do we track this guy down?"

Caleb almost said, *We need Cere.*

"Let's take a ride." Sitting still was making Caleb itchy, restless. He needed to do something, anything, so he wouldn't feel so useless.

What had changed? If Del had been in hiding all these years, why now?

"Is that a good idea, boss?" Rose nodded at Caleb's beer.

"You're welcome to report me to your local sheriff's department." Caleb took another pull before climbing into the truck. Rose hadn't relinquished her beer either. She slid into the middle seat, and Kyle climbed in beside her.

The sky had darkened, and now the stars were out full force. Caleb switched on the high beams and pulled out of the drive. He'd been running Lewis's roads since before he could legally drive. He could probably make the drive with his eyes closed, but tonight he didn't want to miss a thing.

"Where are we going?" Kyle leaned around Rose.

"Back in time." Caleb flicked a glance to the side, seeing Kyle and Rose's concerned expressions. He swallowed the rest of his beer, leaving the bottle to rattle around in the cup holder.

A feeling like lightning crawled under his skin, intensifying as he turned toward his grandparents' old house. His old house, even though he and his father had only lived there for another few months after Cere disappeared. It seemed like another lifetime when he'd belonged to that place. At the same time, remarkably little had changed, like this particular part of Lewis was frozen in time. Caleb knew small, rural towns. In any place other than Lewis, someone would have moved in on an isolated patch of land like Archie Royce's and set up a cook house. Or the government would be after it for timber. It certainly wouldn't be sitting empty.

But this land was tainted and not just with the black rot that had once marked the yard. It was sick down to the roots. Archie Royce had been a monster bad enough to keep all the others away, even now.

Caleb caught himself gripping the wheel and forced himself to relax, slowing to make sure he didn't miss the turn. Trees had grown up, but the old driveway was still visible. Barely. He parked just off the road, retrieving a flashlight from the glove compartment. Kyle pulled his phone out of his pocket, using its flashlight. Neither beam penetrated very far into the darkness.

As Caleb panned his light over the trees, he half-expected eyes to shine back at him. The chirr of insects and the low thump of frogs filled the night. At least those had come back. Maybe that meant whatever hold Archie had over this place was lessening? Caleb held onto that hope as Rose and Kyle followed him down the drive.

Not even the outline of Archie Royce's house remained, but Caleb could still feel it. The last burned timber and cracked stone had been hauled away years ago, the land itself scraped flat, but the sense of a space that had once unfolded to become something much larger continued to haunt the ground. The world was warped here; the trees that had managed to grow in the intervening years kept their distance, preserving the memory of the house like a ghost.

"What are we looking for?" Kyle asked.

"I don't know." The delicate hope in Caleb's chest faltered.

A tiny, foolish part of him had expected to find Cere here waiting for him.

"You have that look," Kyle moved closer, the fingers of his free hand brushed Caleb's arm, a simple touch to reassure them both.

"What look?"

"Like you're about to tell me to wait in the truck or, better yet, go home where I'll be safe." Kyle's lips shaped a half-smile, but Caleb couldn't help wonder if there was an edge of hurt under his words.

Kyle was the very picture of a mid-Western farm boy—blonde hair, blue eyes, shining like the sun over a field of wheat. There was nothing fragile about him, but Caleb couldn't help a complicated impulse to protect him. If they'd been any other place, he wasn't certain he'd feel the same. It was Lewis, its history, the things Caleb had seen here. Archie Royce's legacy was his fight, and he felt a duty to keep Kyle safe from that.

"I would never." Caleb tried to flash a reassuring grin, but it stretched the skin of his face too tight, like a mask. A tiny, nagging voice in the back of his head told him he was being selfish. Despite everything he'd already told him, he was trying to preserve Kyle as the one clean, bright thing in his life, a safe haven to retreat to.

Kyle reached for Caleb's free hand now, squeezing his fingers briefly before letting go. Caleb pushed the ugly thought away.

"Hey, at least I'm finally putting my degree to practical use, right?" Kyle put his arms out to keep his balance as his foot caught a root, and he almost tripped. At the same time, a branch cracked, the sound echoing weirdly.

"Rose?" Caleb swung around.

"Here, boss."

Caleb jumped at the sound of her voice, so close. The sound of the snapping branch had definitely come from farther away. His expression must have changed. Beside him, Rose tensed, her hand going to her hip for a weapon she no longer wore now that she was off-duty.

"Shit."

Caleb hushed her, aiming his flashlight at the trees. Kyle pointed his phone the same way. The beams picked out a shape between two trunks. Catfish John. Caleb couldn't help the thought. But the shape was wrong in a wholly different way. Melted almost. Caleb couldn't think of a better word.

He lowered the light a fraction, holding out his other hand to show he was unarmed.

"Boss . . ." Rose's tone held a warning.

It could be a hunter, maybe there'd been an accident. Or someone who'd gotten drunk and wandered away from their camp. He wanted the rationalizations to be true.

A digital shutter-click broke the stillness, Kyle snapping a picture with his phone. The man—was it a man?—spun, crashing away from them. Caleb plunged after him.

The beam of his flashlight bounced ahead of him, catching stuttering glances of the man's movement. Jerky. Wrong. And it wasn't just the light. Caleb ducked under branches, but the man plowed straight through them.

Just as he started to close the gap, Caleb's foot caught. He went down, swearing as the flashlight flew out of his hand. The beam illuminated the lower half of the man's leg. He was barefoot. In fact, he seemed to be naked, great ropes of scar tissue circling his legs.

"You okay?" Rose caught up, reaching to help him stand.

"Get—" Caleb wheezed, the fall had winded him. He pointed through the trees.

Rose scooped up the flashlight. The man, the creature, whatever, was gone.

"Shit." Caleb managed to get his breathing under control.

"Caleb." Kyle joined them, the alarm in his voice mirrored by his expression. He held his phone out, screen turned to show the picture he'd taken. Maybe it was the camera struggling in the low light, but there was something blurred about the man. Burned. Caleb's first impression of the man as melted returned, stronger, like candle wax dripping and reforming.

"Looks like a bad special effect." Despite the words, Rose's voice held an edge.

"Right?" Kyle turned the phone to look at the screen again. "So, what? Wendigo? Zombie? Bigfoot? Swamp Thing?"

Caleb could almost see him scrolling through mythology textbooks behind his eyes, adding to that copious amounts of science fiction, fantasy, and horror consumed across multiple mediums as a kid.

"That wasn't some dude in a rubber suit," Rose said.

"No." Caleb tested weight on his leg. Tender, but no permanent damage.

It was a moment before he realized Rose and Kyle were looking to him like they expected him to know what to do. And he should. Not just because he was the sheriff but because he'd dragged them into this, and he was the closest thing there was to a expert. Caleb shook his head.

"We're not going to do any good blundering around in the dark. This was a stupid idea in the first place."

He turned, limping slightly as he walked back toward the truck. Rose touched his arm.

"Hey. Don't beat yourself up, boss. It's been a weird day."

Caleb swallowed, throat suddenly thick. It wasn't just Kyle; it was Rose too. The look they'd given, waiting to follow his lead, implied trust. That came with barbs. If he fucked this up, it impacted them too.

Family. The word came unbidden to his mind, and Caleb pushed it away. It was too big to hold right now. He'd lost too many people to Archie Royce, and his shadow still hung over this place. He'd be damned if he lost anyone else.

chapter two

In the summer of 1931, a series of killings took place following a rough line along the Mississippi, from the delta to the bayou. Eight confirmed victims: Theresa Harding, Janet Duplo, Teddy Fishton, Raymond Dante, Eleanor Washington, Helen Elgin, Richard Carter, and Alice Haight. Around the time of the fourth killing, newspapers dubbed the spree the "Catfish Murders" on account of the way the bodies were mutilated post mortem. Each had long cuts made on either side of their throats, like gills, and they were also given reverse Glasgow smiles, the ends of their mouths extended down just like a catfish. The killer was never caught. Just another one of the great mysteries of this area.

—*Myths, History, and Legends from the Delta to the Bayou* (Whippoorwill Press, 2016)

CERE CROUCHED IN THE RUINS OF HER OLD HOUSE, THE WALLS SKETCHED IN lines of black rot staining the ground. With the logic of dreams, she appeared to be five or six years old, younger than Caleb had ever known her. Her mouth moved, but Caleb couldn't understand her. As he reached for her, shadows burst from her skin, lashing around his wrist, pulling him forward.

Caleb jerked, legs kicking to keep himself from falling, tangling in the sheets instead. He turned to see Kyle with one arm tossed over his head, his mouth slightly open. At least he hadn't woken him this time.

Caleb eased out of bed, padding barefoot through the house and out onto the back porch. He'd stayed up for hours after Kyle had gone to bed, skimming through old files of his father's that he'd brought home from the office. Of course, they hadn't revealed anything new, not that he'd expected them to. The sky was still flush with stars, so he couldn't have slept long. Apparently he'd followed in his father's footsteps with regard to insomnia too.

Not for the first time, he considered whether the dead end he ran into at every turn was somehow Catfish John's doing, obscuring himself, obscuring Cere. Caleb stepped off the porch. A faint chill seeped up from the grass through the soles of his feet. If she knew how much he needed her, would Cere come home?

He listened to the rustle of wind through the trees bordering the property, a dog barking. He marked each and let the sounds fall away until there was only his breathing. Once upon a time, he'd called Catfish John, and Catfish John heard him. He didn't have the carving anymore, but maybe Cere would still hear him somehow.

He formed a picture in his mind of the day they'd sat in the back of his father's truck, eating ice cream, their feet swinging from the tailgate. She'd healed him. She might be an apocalypse bound in human form, but she was more than that too.

He reached for the memory of Cere fighting Del, her song, and for Catfish John's song. The notes slipped and twisted away from him, but he understood the feeling. Comfort. Safety. Home. Bracing himself, Caleb sank into the memory of being pressed to the ground, of Cere and Catfish John's music unwinding him, stripping away his flesh and leaving him bare to the stars.

Come home, he thought. *Come home.*

Cere was there, just beyond his reach. If he could only just . . . it was . . .

It was stupid.

Caleb's eyes flew open. A mosquito whined next to his ear; he slapped at it, breaking his concentration. The song, ragged as morning mist burning off over the trees, slipped away. Stupid, stupid, stupid. What had he expected? He crept back into the house. Exhaustion coupled with disappointment swept over him; for the first time in a very long time, had no trouble falling asleep.

The smell of mud and leaf rot. The dusty, rich scent of earth, laid over with still water. Eyes—just visible above the water's surface—watching him. Below the surface lay worse things. A splash put Caleb knee-deep in the brackish water. Another splash. Cere walked toward him. Light coming from her skin and moving eerily over the water as she drew closer. The same age as when he'd last seen her; then she flickered and became a full-grown woman, not pregnant as in his other dreams but thin, muscled, like she'd spent a long time running. Threads of gold snaked through her eyes. She took Caleb's hand in her own, at once large and small—an adult's and a child's.

"We have to go." He didn't see her lips move, but he heard her.

The mud-scent grew stronger, silt and an animal smell. The water surged, a wave slapping him.

"Caleb, now. It's time."

Cere's voice yanked at him. Not inside his dream but . . .

Caleb flailed awake, gasping for air, the second time in how many hours? Cere stood at the foot of the bed, dripping water.

Caleb scrambled backward, reaching for the light. His fingers brushed it, knocking it over. The crash brought Kyle awake, and Caleb instinctively put a hand across his chest, holding him back.

Cere couldn't be here. But she was, no longer wearing a dress clinging to her legs with the weight of mud but jeans and a T-shirt. No water soaked the rug under her feet. She looked fully human, tired and worn.

"Hi," she said.

A simple word, but it landed like a blow. The air left him in a rush.

"Caleb?" Kyle's voice mixed confusion with an edge of fear. Caleb felt an absurd relief that Kyle could see her too.

"It's okay," Caleb said. Was it?

"Are you really here?" He turned his attention back to Cere. His voice came out smaller than he would have liked, his twelve-year-old self watching her disappear into the swamp again.

"Who—" Kyle started and stopped, his eyes widening. "Oh shit."

"I was a long way away, but I came home." A smile touched the corner of Cere's lips, sad, apologetic, acknowledging the inadequacy of her words. But the one word that mattered rang in Caleb's head: *home*.

"Where were you?" Caleb lowered his hand. Kyle put a hand on his arm, steadying him, grounding him. "This is Kyle. He's . . . you can trust him," Caleb said finally.

Cere sat on the edge of the bed but didn't look at either of them full on.

"I went outside." The way she said it, Caleb knew she didn't mean outdoors. "Catfish John took me somewhere my father and brothers couldn't reach me."

A faint tremor shivered Cere's skin, the suggestion that safe wasn't necessarily pleasant.

"You came back." Caleb couldn't help staring at her, still trying to process her presence.

Family left, they died and disappeared, but sometimes they came home again too.

Cere finally turned to look at him. The gold in her eyes looked like fractures now, tiny fissures in glass. The darkness was closer to the surface. Cere was more dangerous than she'd ever been before. And in more danger too.

"Del," Caleb said.

And at the same time, Cere said, "He's trying again."

"Will someone please explain what's going on?" Tension made Kyle's voice sharp.

"Sorry." Caleb turned to him.

"Cere." As she spoke, looking at Kyle, Caleb thought of her offering the name years ago in her smoke-roughened voice.

There was a new hardness to her features, an impatience. She'd been gone, *outside*, for a very long time. Maybe she didn't have the will to shield those around her anymore.

"It's really you." Kyle let out a breath. "What changed? Caleb's been looking for you all these years."

"Catfish John . . . his song is weaker. He's fading. I was outside, and I felt Del looking for me. Then I heard you."

Cere shifted her gaze to Caleb; guilt kicked in his chest. Had he put her in danger?

"How much has Caleb told you?" Cere turned back to Kyle.

"As much as I could remember," Caleb answered, ashamed of the details that had slipped from his mind, even for a minute.

Cere pursed her lips, dismissing his guilt. She addressed them both now. It struck Caleb again how much more willing she was to talk, including Kyle automatically even if it put him at risk. What had it been like for her outside? Had being that long in the dark, or wherever she'd been, worn away her humanity?

"Catfish John protected me," Cere said. "He taught me to protect myself. For a while, it was easy. Without me, there was no point in bringing our father back, so Del went into hiding. I should have come back to finish it long ago. I was . . ."

Cere shook her head. "It doesn't matter. I'm back now."

"What exactly is your brother trying to do?" Kyle asked.

"Bring my father back from the dead. End the world. The usual." A wry smile touched her lips but faded quickly. "All of Del's life, my father only had one concern: making sure I was born and filling me with everything necessary to ensure I birthed the end of the world. It's all Del has ever known. It's all I knew for a long time too."

Her gaze moved to Caleb, and he thought he heard a note of pity in her voice. He tried to picture Del as anything other than a monster, as a little boy, desperate for his father's love. What if he'd had someone like Caleb's father to take him in or someone like Catfish John to guide him?

Would it have changed him? Caleb doubted it. Del had taken what his father had given him, turned it into even more cruelty. He had Archie Royce's fanatic vision but worse. He wanted to see people suffer for the sake of suffering. And he wanted his father there to witness it.

Caleb opened his mouth when something else struck him, a thought that had been nagging at the back of his head. Thinking about Del looking up to his father and the way Ellis had looked up to Del. And Cere had said *brothers* before, not *brother.*

Caleb's pulse quickened.

"We went to your old house last night. We saw something. I think maybe . . . I think Del brought Ellis back with him this time."

"That thing we saw in the woods?" Kyle said.

Cere's shoulders lowered a fraction, but she didn't seem surprised. She closed her eyes, tilting her head back; her whole being flickering. She went from a tired woman sitting on their bed to the woman with glowing skin and a huge belly to the child she had been and then something else entirely. Shadows leaked away from her, a drop of ink spreading in water. Her outline was there, faint, but she unfolded, spreading, growing thinner. Caleb jumped up, and his foot splashed in water. He yanked it back. A swamp filled the room.

"What the hell?" Kyle moved to the center of the bed.

Just as it had arrived, the water vanished. Cere diminished back into herself, opening her eyes.

"Del is stronger now." She spoke as if nothing had happened.

"What do we do?" Caleb asked.

"I'm a monster." Again the sad smile. Cere's eyes were pure gold now like a harvest moon. Her expression changed—unapologetic but not hard. Pragmatic. Caleb wondered again: *what had it been like for her* outside?

"Sometimes you just have to be scarier than the other monsters to win."

Caleb thought of her standing up to Denny Harmon and Robert Lord. It seemed like a lifetime ago. This was different, something completely outside his realm of experience. Except it wasn't. He'd seen her face down Del before. But Del wasn't alone now, and he'd had years to prepare. Then again so had Cere.

"Do you want to understand?"

It was a moment before Caleb realized Cere was talking to Kyle who stared at her wide-eyed.

"Don't." Caleb shifted to put himself between Kyle and Cere, but Kyle moved around him.

"I can make my own decisions." He didn't sound angry, rattled maybe but with curiosity winning out. "If I'm going to help, I want to know."

Cere reached for Kyle's hand, her fingers hovering just short of touching him. Her inhuman eyes asked for certainty one last time, and Kyle nodded. Cere took his hand, pressing it against the flat of her belly.

Flat but with potential. All those nightmares her father wanted her to birth, monsters that would wipe clean the earth. Kyle sucked in a breath. Caleb tensed, waiting for blood to pour from Kyle's nose, but it didn't. His nostrils flared, and the tendons in his neck strained but nothing else. Cere let go of his hand.

It took a moment for his eyes to focus, and when they did, he looked at Cere. Caleb saw a new respect—the kind of respect one would have for a poisonous snake. Kyle stood, brushing his hands on the boxers he slept in as if to wipe away the traces of what Cere had shown him.

"You'll stay with us." It wasn't a question. "I'll make up the guest room."

Caleb's heart flipped, squeezing tight. Just like that, despite what Cere had shown him, Kyle had accepted her, was willing to take her in. Just like he hadn't hesitated to say, *If I'm going to help . . .*

"I don't deserve him." His cheeks warmed as he realized he spoken out loud.

Cere tilted her head to one side, the shadows lifting from her expression. For a moment, Caleb could pretend she really was his sister come home to visit after a long time.

"What makes you say that?"

"All this." Caleb waved vaguely. "It's . . ."

"A lot?"

Caleb nodded and immediately felt guilty. If he was having trouble coping, how must Cere feel? She'd been outside the world. She seemed less human than ever and wearier of trying to hide it. She'd let nightmares slip from her skin so that Kyle could see what she was, what she might be. How much longer could she hold it in?

"What happened to you?" he asked softly.

Cere shifted closer to him and laced her fingers through his, resting her head on his shoulder.

"Catfish John taught me songs to calm the darkness, to make me stronger. And I had this."

With her free hand, she reached into her pocket—a pocket nowhere near big enough to hold it—and drew out the wooden carving.

"It kept me safe. It helped me focus on being human when I wasn't."

The light caught the tangle of wood. Caleb heard a faint, reverberating note. He touched the carving with one finger, and it shivered. The wood resolved for just a moment—Catfish John's face unmistakable.

"What is he?" Caleb asked.

"Very old," Cere said, without lifting her head, as if that were all the answer or explanation needed.

Silence stretched around them. The sound of night insects filtered in even though the window was closed. She slipped the carving back into her pocket. Except no. Caleb knew there was no way the carving would fit in the pocket of her jeans. She'd made it vanish back to the same place she'd drawn it from. Outside.

"Sometimes I'm already there in the dark." Cere's voice was almost inaudible. Caleb flinched but didn't let go of her hand. "I'm there, and I've already birthed monsters, and it's too late to stop it. But I'm here too. Everything is happening all at once."

"The spare room is ready." Kyle stood uncertainly in the doorway.

"Thank you." Cere unfolded herself from the bed.

She touched Kyle's arm in passing and continued down the hall. Kyle took Cere's place on the bed. After a moment, his fingers replaced hers in Caleb's hand.

"Are you okay?" They spoke it at the same time. Caleb laughed, a release of nervous tension.

"Yeah," Caleb said. "You?"

"I think so." Kyle glanced toward the door. "Is she safe?"

Caleb wasn't sure whether Kyle was asking whether Cere was protected or whether they were safe from her.

"I honestly don't know." He answered both.

"So what do we do?" Kyle asked.

"Tomorrow we talk to Rose. Then the four of us sit down together, and . . . we'll figure something out."

The answer was inadequate, but it was all he had. Kyle was putting his trust in Caleb, and the best Caleb could come up with was *we'll figure it out.*

"You don't have—" Caleb started, but Kyle held up his hand.

"Are you kidding? This will make a hell of a thesis paper." Kyle grinned, but catching Caleb's expression, the smile vanished. "Hey," Kyle said, and the knot of tension at his first words released its hold on Caleb, but the lingering fear remained.

"I don't want to be just some story to you. All this . . ." Caleb waved his free hand. "This is my life. Cere's life."

Kyle caught Caleb's other hand and held it too. The gentle pressure of his fingers demanded Caleb's full attention.

"I'm sorry. I was just joking around. It's . . ."

"A lot." Caleb echoed Cere's words.

Kyle nodded. Caleb could almost see him ordering his words before speaking again.

"Look, I know this is . . . big. But I really do want to help, and I know you won't ask. You're damn stubborn that way."

Caleb's throat tightened. His words had already proved inadequate, so he didn't bother, pressing his mouth to Kyle's instead. All the tension and strangeness of the past few days poured out in the kiss. Maybe he'd regret it tomorrow, but for now, the only thing he wanted was Kyle close to him, and he wouldn't suggest leaving again for anything in the world.

chapter three

My daddy used to tell a story about a man who came to town, when he was a boy. Name of Reverend Rice, Reese, something like that. Said he'd come to save folks from the devil. He put up a big revival tent, invited everyone, but no one showed. Well, the reverend got all in a huff, left town saying they were all damned. Ten years later, another man comes to town calling himself the same name. Could have been the first man's brother, maybe even his son.

Since the first reverend left, there'd been a string of murders all the way down to New Orleans. Not just that. A whole mess of frogs came up out of the creek, filled up the roads, got on people's porches, under their doors, into their beds and pantries and everything. Whole flocks of birds dropped dead out of the sky. No one doubted the devil anymore. You can bet the whole town showed up for the reverend's sermon that day and any day after he cared to preach.

—*Myths, History, and Legends from the Delta to the Bayou* (Whippoorwill Press, 2016)

"Del." Cere clenched her jaw; her tone removed any lingering doubt Caleb might have had about the man in Holly DuBois's picture.

Caleb, Cere, and Rose clustered behind Caleb's desk, looking at his laptop. Kyle slumped in one of the visitor chairs, restlessly playing with his phone. Cere wrapped her arms around her upper body, glaring at Del on the screen. Rose slipped out of the room and returned with a steaming cup of coffee.

"It's not great, but it's better than nothing." She handed it to Cere.

Caleb had made the introductions, but Cere hadn't offered to touch Rose the way she had Kyle. Even so, Rose seemed to recognize something in Cere, and the look she gave Caleb was one of reproach—like *why didn't you tell me about this sooner?* He would *definitely* have to ask Rose about her war stories when all this was done. Assuming they survived.

A knock sounded at the door, and Rose stuck her head out into the hall. A feeling of dread crept over Caleb, worsened by Rose's expression as she stepped back into the room.

"Wilson just got back from checking out Pine View. You were right, someone dug up Ellis Royce's grave."

"Jesus." Caleb pinched the bridge of his nose. After sharing his suspicion with Cere last night, he'd sent one of his officers to check the cemetery first thing this morning.

He'd been expecting the result, but being right didn't make him feel better. He could picture the grave. He'd visited it a few times, part of the ritual of reminding himself of everything that had happened. It stood on the edge of the cemetery, half-hidden by a shaggy pine. Caleb had never seen any evidence of anyone besides himself visiting. If he hadn't sent Wilson to check, the dug-up earth might not have been noticed for weeks.

"So that thing we saw in the woods really was a zombie?" Kyle sat up. "Like not in the classic sense but in the *Walking Dead* sense?"

"My daddy's magic." Cere's voice was grim.

Caleb remembered when she'd thought she could reason with Ellis because he wasn't like her father or Del. Had that sympathy burned away outside too?

"Is that why Holly died?" At Rose's voice, Caleb looked up.

"Shit. I'm sorry." He kept forgetting Rose had known her.

The ache between his eyes grew. He thought again of his father, trying to shelter everyone, shoulder the burden alone. As far as following in his footsteps in that sense, Caleb was doing a shit job.

"We have to find him," Cere said.

Caleb wasn't sure whether she was talking about Ellis or Del, but it scarcely mattered. Del had evaded death twice now; Ellis had literally been returned from the grave. Now both were roaming Lewis. His town.

Caleb's whole body felt sore, pummeled, and he wanted to sleep for a week. He squared his shoulders.

"Okay. We'll start at the cemetery."

Caleb sat on the edge of the bed, trying to be as quiet as possible. Kyle spoke without rolling over.

"Everything okay?"

"Okay as it can be with a grave-robbing killer on the loose." He'd spent the last hour listlessly flipping through channels on the TV, trying to shut off his brain, so he could sleep. It hadn't worked.

Pine View Cemetery had been another dead end as were all the other haunts Cere could think of where Del and Ellis might hide. The entire day felt like a wild goose chase, and while they ran around after their own tails, Caleb hadn't been able to shake the feeling Del was somewhere just out of sight, laughing at them.

"Sorry." Caleb breathed out. "Are you okay? How's Cere?"

"Asleep," Kyle said. "I presume."

"Mpf." Caleb let himself collapse onto the bed.

He closed his eyes, knowing sleep wouldn't come despite his bone-deep exhaustion. It wasn't even a moment before the sound of shattering glass jerked him upright. Caleb stood, his pulse tripping double time, and grabbed the Glock from the holster slung over the back of a chair. Kyle followed him down the hall.

"Cere?" Caleb paused outside her door, pistol braced.

She didn't answer. Caleb switched to a one-handed grip, opening the door with his free hand. The grey, melted creature from the woods had an arm wrapped around Cere's throat, dragging her toward the window where spikes of broken glass clung to the sill.

"Shit." He had no clear shot.

Caleb lowered his gun. Without turning his head, he spoke to Kyle over his shoulder, hoping to hell the creature that had been Ellis Royce was far enough gone he couldn't understand him.

"Get my baseball bat from the hall."

The creature cocked its head, but its slack, grey face showed no signs of comprehension. Kyle retreated into the hall. Caleb lifted his pistol again, but he still couldn't get a clear shot. Cere dug her fingers into the arm wrapped around her throat. Chunks of flesh peeled off under her nails, but the grip didn't slacken. That thing was Cere's brother. The thought clanged against the logical part of

Caleb's mind, rolling around in his skull.

In the face of impossibility, Caleb fixed on the solidity of Ellis. Shouldn't he be rotted away by now? Was that more of Archie Royce's magic? He pictured Archie or Del slowly poisoning Ellis over the years, not just his mind but his body, preparing him to become something else after death. A tool for them to use. As his mind spun on useless thoughts, Cere twisted in Ellis's grip, speaking a word that turned the air black. Shadows writhed, and then suddenly she was in front of Caleb, her back to him like a shield.

The creature lunged, and Cere shoved Caleb backward. The air thickened until he could barely see Cere or Ellis. Then Cere's voice rang out, and the fog vanished.

Kyle stood in front of Caleb, holding the aluminum baseball bat. Cere had managed to back them into the kitchen, but the thing that had been Ellis had followed them. It made a clumsy swipe for the bat.

Caleb threw himself forward with a shout, catching Ellis around the knees. They hit the ground, rolling together and crashing into the wall. Ellis ended up on top, straddling him, dead weight holding Caleb down.

Caleb finally got a good look at Ellis and wished he hadn't. Ellis's eye sockets were empty, but within the darkness, there was still a kind of intent, malicious and pained like a whipped dog driven mad with hurt. Ellis's skin was grey ash, the remains of a campfire with the embers burned out. Amongst the burnt ruin, Caleb caught sight of pale scars, older markings. He thought again of Archie Royce preparing Ellis over the years, and sickness rose in the back of his throat. Ellis, Del, Cere—maybe the children who'd died had been the lucky ones.

It was a sickening thought, and it sent a fresh surge of anger through him. Caleb clawed at Ellis's arms, and a strip of flesh tore away, revealing ivory bone. Ellis didn't falter, his grip impossibly strong as he wrapped his hands around Caleb's throat. He leaned his weight forward, pressing on Caleb's windpipe.

Black spots burst in front of Caleb's eyes, his ears roaring. He pawed at the hands holding him down, but he couldn't get a grip. He thought of Kyle, his father, Cere, all the people he'd let down. All at once, the pressure vanished, and Ellis slumped sideways. Cere stood over them. A tendril of solid darkness, like smoke, folded itself back into her body.

A gaping hole in the center of Ellis's chest showed splinters of bone but nothing wet; all the meat had burned away years ago. Cere had punched right through him.

"Oh fuck." Caleb scrambled to his feet.

Kyle reached them, throwing his arms around Caleb so hard Caleb wheezed.

"Sorry." Kyle let go. "Are you okay?"

Caleb nodded. He touched his throat. Tomorrow it would be bruised.

"You?"

Kyle nodded. He kept an arm around Caleb's waist as Cere knelt beside the remains of her brother.

"I didn't want it to be him." Cere's expression was complicated, caught between pity and looking like she wanted to spit on the corpse. "Del made him into a monster long before he made him into *this*." Cere nudged Ellis's corpse with her foot.

"We'll find Del." Caleb's voice was strained; his throat hurt. "I've got every available officer out looking."

"It won't be enough." Cere looked Caleb square in the eye. "If he doesn't want to be found, he won't be. I think he's got someplace like the outside he can step into. Not the same place Catfish John took me, but someplace he can disappear."

Even though she was real and solid, standing in front of him, Caleb could still see the ghost-image of Cere from his dreams, a second self inside her skin. If it came to it, if it looked like Del was going to win, he knew what she would do. Cere crouched, slipping her arms under Ellis's body.

"What are you doing?"

Cere shot him a look of impatience.

"Taking care of things."

"I have to call it in." Even as he said it, the idea of trying to explain Ellis's death, re-death, seemed absurd.

"Ellis has been dead for years." Cere's gaze pinned him. "His death certificate is on file."

"So what, we—"

"We burn the body, close up the grave in Pine View, and you write whatever you want in your report."

Cere's tone left no room for argument. Caleb thought of a conversation with his father a lifetime ago. He was in his father's shoes now, arguing the side of the law. But that position only held if the world made sense, and right now, it didn't.

Kyle leaned against him, not saying anything but adding the solid comfort of his presence. Caleb took a deep breath. Whatever he'd professed to believe aloud, his father had still taken Cere in, smelling like ash, and never questioned how the fire started. He'd seen a girl who'd never had anything but hate to raise her, and he'd done everything he could to fill the hole where her family should have been. For all of his principles, his father had held one truth higher—family was bigger than the law.

"Okay," Caleb said. "We'll follow your lead. Tell us what we need to do."

"We need to take Ellis home. Finish this where it started."

chapter four

They burned him, hanged him, shot him. They even slit his throat and strung him up by his ankles, left him swinging from a tree for the crows to pick, left his fingers trailing in the water for the fish to eat. In every story I ever heard about Catfish John, he died. Painfully. Violently. Sometimes he was a monster, but sometimes, he was just a man.

—*Myths, History, and Legends from the Delta to the Bayou* (Whippoorwill Press, 2016)

Rose parked behind Caleb. He'd called her before they left, feeling guilty doing so but wanting her by their side. The wash of her headlights illuminated the tarp-wrapped bundle in the bed of Caleb's truck before she killed the engine and climbed out of her car. Even in the dark, Caleb didn't miss the grim set of her jaw.

"I deserve a raise for this. And a promotion."

"You gunning for my job? You're welcome to it."

The four of them stood in silence, listening to the tick of cooling engines and the chorus of night insects.

"Let's get this over with." Caleb wiped his hands on his jeans and lowered the tailgate.

Ellis's body was surprisingly light as though whatever Del had done to bring him back had hollowed him out. Caleb climbed into the truck bed, and between the four of them, they wrestled the awkward bundle to the razed remains of Archie Royce's house, just an empty patch of land now.

"Here." Cere pointed. "It was his room."

Caleb wondered how she could tell, but of course, the house she'd been imprisoned in would be imprinted on her just the same as Archie Royce's magic. As they carried his body, Caleb tried to picture Ellis as a child. Cere had said Ellis had been kind to her once. Maybe he'd even tried to protect her before Archie and Del killed every kind impulse in him.

He helped Cere unwrap the body while Rose and Kyle stepped back. The stars looked down on them, bright and unforgiving.

"He always wanted to be like Del." Cere's tone was thoughtful. "Even when he hated him, he looked up to him. He deserves better, but I want Del to see. If he wants me, he needs to do his own dirty work."

Cere's lips peeled back from her teeth, a feral, pained expression. Under it, there was loss. The one thing that had the potential to be good in her life, and it had been corrupted and taken away from her. Caleb joined Kyle and Rose.

Cere remained beside Ellis's body, head bowed in concentration. After a moment, the air around her changed, wavering. Shadows curled around her like grey-black flames.

Kyle tensed, and Rose moved toward Cere, but Caleb put a hand on her arm. Light flickered between Cere's fingers. She touched them to Ellis's body, and he burst into flame.

"Jesus!" Heat bloomed toward them, and Caleb and Kyle both stepped back.

"She's going to kill herself." Rose tried to shake Caleb off.

"Wait." Caleb tightened his grip on Rose's arm. His pulse hammered, but he trusted Cere. "She knows what she's doing."

Cere tipped her head back, keeping her hands pressed to Ellis's body inside the fire but remaining unburned. Caleb felt the sound before he properly heard it—a low hum rising to something that wasn't quite music. It was the lullaby Catfish John had sung the night he took Cere away. It was the mourning sound he'd heard Cere make, a keening wail and a soothing hush all at once.

Caleb put his arm around Rose's shoulders. He slid his other arm around Kyle's waist. He almost bowed his head, but in the end, he settled for silently wishing for peace—for Ellis, for Cere, for them all.

Cere lifted her hands, shaking free droplets of pale fire that sizzled and vanished into the dark. Where Ellis had lain, only a pile of ash remained. A cry split the air—a bird, a wild animal in pain, a soul in torment. Caleb pulled Rose and Kyle closer.

"What the hell was that?" Kyle asked.

"Del knows what I did." New lines of exhaustion etched Cere's mouth, and shadows darkened her eyes. Reluctantly Caleb let go of Kyle and Rose, reaching to help Cere up, but she shook her head.

"I'm staying here. I'll watch until dawn." Seeing the doubt that must have been in Caleb's eyes, she continued. "He won't be able to touch me."

Cere dipped a finger in her brother's ashes, sketching symbols in the dirt around her. When she was finished, she spit in the ash and drew on her skin as well.

"This is his place of power. I'm taking it back."

"What do we—" Caleb started, but Cere shook her head again.

"Go home. Get some rest. We'll need to be ready for Del tomorrow."

She shifted to sit cross-legged, closing her eyes and resting her hands on her knees. She might have been a statue, a ghost, ash-smeared in the darkness. She was a young girl, all knobby knees and fresh from the burned remains of her home. She was the light of a star and the end of the world in the shape of a woman.

Caleb opened his mouth but closed it again. There was nothing else to say.

"I'll make hot tea." Rose followed Caleb and Kyle inside. "I doubt any of us are sleeping. We might as well keep each other company."

Exhaustion and adrenaline warred in Caleb's system. He slumped into a chair, putting his hand over his eyes. When Rose returned with the tea, Kyle pulled a bottle of brandy out of the cabinet and added a measure to each of their mugs.

"What the hell just happened? Really." Kyle wrapped his hands around his tea. "What did we see? I mean it's one thing to read Frazer, but it's another to see a woman set fire to the corpse of her brother with her bare hands."

From down the hall, the plastic Caleb had hastily taped over Cere's shattered window rattled. Leaving aside his tea, he retrieved another glass and poured himself a straight measure of brandy. He didn't have answers for Kyle, for himself even.

As he took a swallow, a stray memory flitted across Caleb's mind of Jayleen Culligan's bicycle, stolen from outside Lewis Middle School during basketball practice. She'd come into the sheriff's office, clearly upset but putting on her bravest and most serious face, to make her report. Caleb had set aside his work to help her track the bike down himself. The look on her face when they'd finally found it had been pure magic.

He wasn't his daddy. Maybe not everyone in Lewis liked him, but he could be a damn good sheriff, and he wasn't going to sit around and wait, hoping Del would show up. They had one resource he hadn't tried yet—Catfish John. Caleb wasn't going to let him sulk in his swamp anymore. He was going to drag him out and make him help Cere.

He stood. Rose and Kyle exchanged a look and followed him down the hall to the guest room. The plastic flapped in the wind again.

"What are you—" Kyle started, but Caleb held up a hand.

He was twelve years old again. The carving had been there then when he needed it; it would be here again now. This was what passed for truth in a world that didn't make sense. Magic. He just had to believe it.

Caleb closed his eyes, concentrating until he felt a shivering sensation in his bones. Music on the edge of hearing. His fingertips brushed the bedside table and passed beyond it. *Through.* Caleb sucked in a breath, plunging his hand into icy water so cold it burned. As his fingers closed, the slick shape of the carved wood became something else. It writhed, a mass of living things, like trying to hold onto a handful of eels. The song turned deafening. There was a sharp stab of pain like something had bitten him, but he refused to let go.

The squirming stopped, and Caleb yanked his hand free. There was a soft pop like a light bulb breaking, and the world rushed back in with a clamor of voices, Rose and Kyle overlapping each other in alarm.

"—we can't just let him—"

"—I don't want to hurt—"

Rose had a grip on his elbow, but she let go as he turned to face her.

"What the actual fuck?" She stared at him.

"What?" Caleb looked between them. Kyle's face was ashen.

"You just . . ." Kyle paused, swallowed. "You just sort of reached into thin air. Your hand"—he pointed—"was gone."

Caleb looked at his hand, gripping Cere's carving. He had a vague recollection of Rose trying to yank his arm out of the nothingness, reliving the past few moments from a different perspective, two realities slightly askew.

"What the fuck is that thing?" Rose pointed.

"It's our key to finding Catfish John."

The sky was still dark, just thinking about turning blue-grey as Caleb pulled off the road and parked the car. Even though the sun wasn't up, heat lingered behind the skin of night, waiting to break. Sweat nagged at the back of his neck and under his arms. Maybe when this was all over, he and Kyle would finally leave Lewis. It wasn't the first time the thought had occurred to him, but until now, leaving had never seemed feasible. Whether he admitted it or not, all this time he'd been waiting for Cere to return, for Del and Archie to finish what they'd started.

He glanced at Rose as she came around the front of the car. What would she do if he left? Likely take over the department and run things better than he could. Caleb snorted, catching himself too late.

"Something funny, boss?"

"Nothing. Long night." He pulled the flashlight from his belt, aiming it into the trees.

Caleb started down the incline, Rose and Kyle following. He glanced over his shoulder as their feet crunched over fallen branches. Déjà vu. He kept dragging them on wild-goose chases in the dark. If anything happened to either of them . . .

"With all due respect, boss man, shut up."

Caleb startled as Rose spoke.

"I didn't say anything."

"Didn't have to. You were thinking it loud enough to wake the whole damn woods."

"You were going to tell us we don't have to come with you," Kyle said.

"For the thousandth time," Rose added.

"We know the risks."

"So again," Rose said, "due respect, but shut it."

"But what if—" Caleb started, unable to help himself.

Rose stopped, pointing her flashlight so it blinded him temporarily. He blinked away grey spots as she lowered it. Her expression was one he'd never seen before.

"This ain't my first rodeo." Rose flashed the edge of a grin. "My granny taught me everything she knew."

"War stories?" Caleb raised an eyebrow.

"Oh yeah." Rose grinned.

She pointed her flashlight straight ahead again, striding past Caleb. Kyle hurried to catch up.

"I'm definitely going to be there for that conversation. I might even get two thesis papers out of this."

"Then we all better make damn sure we survive." Caleb followed them.

The sky turned pale grey, the ground softening. Light reflected off water, coming back from Caleb's flashlight, and he switched it off. Patches of wetness appeared ahead, trunks rising from the mud.

Further on, the land gave way to pure water, the swamp proper. But here, they were in-between. A liminal space where anything could exist—even a monster.

He'd wrapped Cere's carving in a cloth, tucked it into the bag he carried slung over his shoulder. Caleb unwrapped it now, feeling it buzz and shiver as he did. He thrust it out like a dowsing rod as he'd seen Cere do once a long time ago.

"Catfish John!"

Something far out in the swamp rolled over, a massive creature turning in its sleep. A spike of fear shot through Caleb, but he tamped it down. Around the carving, his palm dampened with sweat. He licked his lips and tried again.

"I have your song. The one you gave Cere. She needs your help."

Movement. A light reflecting in the water like a will-o-wisp.

"Hey!" Caleb plunged forward.

Mud splashed his legs, and the ground sucked at his feet. He slipped, catching himself with an arm that sunk to the elbow. The air smelled of rotting things. A faintly metallic smell. Caleb pushed himself up, tossing the flashlight away. Screw it.

When he straightened, Catfish John stood in front of him as though he'd solidified out of the heavy pre-dawn air. Caleb swallowed a shout.

"Cere needs your help. Please." Caleb found his voice.

He was close enough to touch, but Caleb still couldn't see Catfish John properly. It was as though the man—or whatever he was—bent the light around himself, refusing Caleb's gaze. Caleb could only see him in fragments, pieces of an impossible puzzle: a downturned mouth, glossy black eyes, grey skin that had a sheen to it like a pigeon's wing.

Caleb briefly had the impression that an actual fish stood reared up on its tail, nine feet tall, with a mouth wide enough to swallow him whole. In the next instant, Catfish John was just a man, his skin mottled and pale. A shadow traced the line of his jaw, gills, or a scar.

All the stories he and Kyle had tracked down, the legends and folktales and songs passed down from generation to generation. A lost god, an exiled devil, a simple man who'd outlived his natural lifespan. In this moment, he could easily believe all of the accounts were true. How many of the stories were seeds sown by Catfish John himself? Myth as camouflage to keep himself hidden?

Archie Royce had dedicated his life to destroying Catfish John like his father before him and so on back. But it wasn't wickedness Caleb saw in those infinitely black eyes, only grief, inexplicable loss, loneliness.

"I'm sorry." Caleb stretched out his hand. It hovered in the space between them.

Catfish John shook his head. Caleb could see a little of what Cere had been talking about. Catfish John was thin in places, almost translucent. There were cracks, holes where strange stars showed through.

"I waited for her."

Caleb wasn't sure whether he heard the words or simply imagined them. Catfish John's lips didn't seem to move, but Caleb understood nonetheless. He saw a line of shadowy figures, Archie Royce and his kin. Each iteration grew more blurred, more fractured. A whole line dedicated to hate, to destruction. And Cere, the bright spot at the end.

Catfish John's story was inextricably linked with the Royces. If he hadn't existed, would they have willed him into being to have something to fight? Something to loathe? Whatever he was, Catfish John blamed himself; Caleb could see it.

"There must be something I can do." Caleb's hand remained in the air between them. The rest of the world had dropped away. There was only Catfish John.

Another shake of his head. There were volumes in Catfish John's motion—it said *not yet* and *too late* and maybe even *never*. Startled, Caleb dropped his hand. A spike of pure cold shot through him, his heart breaking.

"If we help Cere, if we stop Archie and Del, then no one will be hunting you.

You can disappear. We can tell more stories to help you hide, throw people off your trail." Caleb realized he was babbling.

He glanced over his shoulder, but he couldn't see Kyle and Rose. He tried not to picture them frantically searching for him, hearing their distorted, panicked voices as they'd tried to pull his arm free from the hole in the world.

Catfish John's voice, or the idea of it, came again—low and sonorous like the swamp itself speaking to Caleb's bones. At the same time, it was a strained whisper from a wounded throat.

"She already burns."

Catfish John pointed. The webbed skin joining his fingers glistened. Caleb saw the sky brighten, not sunrise but a glow like flames.

His breath stuttered.

"Cere."

Of course, she'd done it again, sent him away, so she could fight Del on her own. How could he have been so stupid? Light shifted through Catfish John's eyes, galaxies unfurling. Caleb held his breath—an instant, a lifetime.

"Her song."

For a moment, Caleb could only stare, uncomprehending, and then he remembered the figurine clutched in his hands. He held it out. Catfish John touched the carving with one finger.

The song—universes dying and being born and the stars so bright so cold so beautiful—slammed into Caleb. It took his breath away, consuming him until it was everything. It shredded him, and for a moment, Caleb wanted nothing more than to let go, let the music unweave him and scatter him. But . . .

Cere.

He sucked in a breath. It burned all the way down. The swamp spread around him; he could feel it, trees stretching up to the sky, roots sunk deep in the water. Beyond that, Lewis. He could see all of it, hold it all in his hand, and it was so small. The earth spun, and everywhere else was dark and stars and . . . oh.

Space and time folded around him. He thought of Kyle and Rose, cast their names like a net into the screaming dark, snagging them and pulling them with him.

Caleb hit the ground on his hands and knees, gasping for breath. In the dark, in-between, he'd seen the things from Cere's visions, her reality. Just beyond his reach. They existed, a breath away from the everyday world he knew.

Rose and Kyle knelt beside him. They were back on Archie Royce's land, and all around them, the world burned.

"Holy shit!" Rose scrambled up.

Caleb stood, catching her as she took a step and plunged into water up to the knee. He yanked her back. All around the place where Archie Royce's house had stood, the ground had turned to swamp, mud-brown waters reflecting the burning sky. A scaled back broke the water, something impossibly long turning without quite surfacing.

"Shit shit shit." Rose gripped Caleb's arm, and Caleb reached for Kyle with his other arm, needing the reassurance of him.

"We have to get to Cere." A burning wind whipped past them, heavy with ash. Caleb had to shout to be heard.

Strips of sky peeled away. Like Ellis Royce's skin sloughing away beneath Caleb's fingers.

"Cere!" Caleb shouted into the maelstrom.

Something thrashed in the water behind them, but he refused to turn. The phantom walls of a burned house flickered into existence, past and present collapsing into one. Caleb tripped over a burnt beam that wasn't there, and Kyle helped him to his feet.

"Cere!"

A low sound like thunder, rising to a growl. An animal sound. A bone-cracking sound. Lightning shivered across the not-sky, illuminating trees filled with bodies hanging by their ankles, fingers trailing in the swamp for the creatures there to feed.

"Over there." Kyle pointed.

The wet, tearing sound continued, growing louder, becoming a roar. There were words in it, low and guttural. It was a moment before Caleb realized it was a human voice speaking but in a way no human voice should.

Caleb could just make out a figure. Swollen, too large for the confines of its flesh. One moment, it was emaciated, its matted black hair streaked with grey. The next, it unfolded, a monstrous head scraping the sky, red and black and lightning-struck. A sick-yellow eye rolled and glared at them. Teeth like broken tombstones, and limbs that folded and bent in the wrong way, too many of them, reaching outside and inside the world all at once.

A manifestation of Del and Archie Royce melded into one terrible being.

The wind pushing at them vanished, and Caleb stumbled.

The sudden silence only lasted a moment, and then the world roared at them. Caleb clapped his hands over his ears, twelve years old again. Utter darkness swamped him. He lost track of Kyle and Rose; panic slammed through him. He was facedown in the mud, breathing the swamp, drowning.

He tried to shout their names and drew in a lungful of silt instead. He coughed, choking, and then his vision cleared. He pushed himself upright.

The real Del Royce crouched over his father's body. Like Ellis, Archie should have rotted years ago, but the corpse was fresh, unnaturally preserved. Despite the stiff, waxen color of his skin, at any moment he might open his eyes. When he did, they would be ivory, twin to the monstrous eye rolling in the sky above father and son.

Del had made himself into a cage of flesh, a conduit. The thing warping and changing his body, growing new dimensions and brushing against the sky, that was Archie waking up, coming home.

"Caleb!" Caleb turned to see Kyle pinned to the earth by an invisible force, struggling to raise one arm to point at something just beyond Archie Royce's body.

Cere.

Caleb jerked toward her without actually moving, a kick in his chest, a scream wanting to break free. A glow clung to her skin, and her body rose, hanging in the air. She made a faint sound like someone trying to wake from a bad dream. Relief and anger flooded through him. Cere was alive, but she was clearly in pain.

"What did you do to her?" He ground out the words, each one a stone pushed out of his throat.

Del ignored him, speaking words that stuttered like thunder. His body rocked, and the thing that was Archie Royce twisted above him. Had he ever been human? Caleb wanted to squeeze his eyes shut, but he couldn't. Words that weren't words buzzed and crawled against his skin.

Turning slowly in the air, Cere's body twitched. All the memories Archie had forced into her poured back out, feeding him. A woman with pale skin screamed her birth pains, filling the air with the coppery-thick scent of blood. Her body rotted, decomposing into the swamp. The air sizzled, ozone, a storm trapped inside dank, fetid walls. Another woman now, holding a squalling newborn against her body, fighting as Archie ripped it from her and smashed its skull against a stone.

How many bones in the swamp? How many babies smothered or crushed or drowned until Cere was born? Caleb shook, fighting the horror of it. Cere rose higher, her limbs slack. She was a little girl, a grown woman, a goddess swollen with the light of the moon.

She struggled, fighting to hold on, to hold darkness in. Her eyes snapped open. Their gold struck Caleb like a blow. Her lips moved.

"Stop him."

He struggled upright, even as the world tried to crush him. He took a step, feet dragging. Cere flickered, blurred, became shadows bleeding out from the center, tendrils of darkness curling outward and wrapping around everything. The tendrils snapped trees, ripped their roots from the earth, filling the air with the sound of splintering wood. She spoke again, and the words cracked against Caleb's heart.

"Stop me."

He gritted his teeth, forcing himself to take another step. He couldn't raise his head, not all the way. Del seemed unaware of him, his body still jerking as though in a trance, words pouring out of him, speaking themselves through him.

By the light from Cere's skin, Caleb could see symbols carved onto Archie Royce's arms, his chest, his cheeks. They covered his body, flaring dark, pulsing. Caleb flung himself forward. It took every last ounce of his strength, the motion more like falling. The world became an abyss, and he tipped himself into it.

Kyle shouted behind him. Rose's voice was there too. Both came from very far away, slowed down and stretched until the moment of impact. He struck Del, knocking him sideways.

Like a door slamming shut, Del crashed back into himself, something huge crammed into a tiny space. He snarled, snapping rotten teeth at Caleb. Caleb jerked back, fighting to get free as he had fought to get closer a moment before. Age had ravaged Del's face, but it was more than that. The humanity had drained from him, whatever little he'd had, leaving a hollow mask. Only his singular purpose remained—end the world and thereby end Catfish John.

Del wrapped his arms around Caleb, pinning him, a wild animal, all strength and rage. He caught a glimpse of Cere as he tried to wriggle free of Del's hold.

He could only hope he'd been able to break Del's concentration enough for her to get free.

"Fight it," Caleb shouted.

Del squeezed, a snake, slowly and inexorably crushing Caleb. An alligator performing a death roll. Caleb's ribs creaked; black spots danced in front of his eyes.

Caleb reached frantically, trying to catch the threads of Catfish John's song. This time, the wooden carving leapt to him. Caleb closed his hand, electricity crackling between his bones.

He couldn't throw the carving; Del had him pinned. He nudged it, felt it roll out of his grip. Hopefully Cere would see or Kyle or Rose. The world dimmed, wanting to go black. He had to get to Kyle. He had to . . .

Singing. He felt it like he'd felt the guttural terrible words calling Archie back from the dead. Except this music lifted him. It put air in his lungs, and he gasped, drawing in an aching breath and coughing it out again. Del froze, grip slackening, and it was enough, so Caleb could wiggle free.

"Caleb." Hands steadied him, and Kyle's voice was next to his ear.

"Don't you dare leave me with this mess, boss. You have to get up. Now." Rose's voice too.

The sky overhead flickered. Rose and Kyle leaned over him. Kyle held his hand, squeezing it hard enough to shift his bones.

"The figurine, get it to Cere." He moved his head, trying to indicate where it had fallen.

He could just see Del out of the corner of his eye, half crouched, an animal trying not to become prey. Rose stood, fingers curled at her side. She darted forward and snatched the figurine. Del snarled, fighting loose of the lullaby.

Caleb stood, leaning on Kyle. Fear locked his throat as Del leapt toward Rose, but she was faster, closing the space between her and Cere and pushing the figurine into Cere's hands where she hung in the air.

A howl shook the sky. The earth cracked, heaving under them, and Caleb lost his balance again. He caught at Kyle, and they held each other up as the ground rocked. The song, coming from everywhere and nowhere, changed, rising. Something so large he couldn't take it in all at once launched itself from the water surrounding them. Crooked jaws, dripping thick-plated armor, powerful limbs, and teeth.

The creature twisted in mid-air, unfolding. A downturn to its mouth, slick greyish skin. Eyes as black as all the space between the stars. Caleb's breath snagged.

The creature's jaws snapped closed, catching Del before it slammed back into the water, sending a wave of brackish filth over them. Caleb tightened his grip on Kyle, clinging as his feet slid in the mud. The sky continued to come apart overhead, the land crumbling underneath them.

Kyle shouted his name. Caleb blinked. Time sped up again. Rose was just now ducking past Cere. And Cere's fingers closed on the figurine. The light emanating from her skin was near unbearable, and Caleb had to shade his eyes.

The singing grew louder, the lullaby steadying Cere. Her form solidified; she stopped turning, stopped drifting. Her feet touched the ground. For a moment, Caleb saw her elsewhere, outside the world in the vast dark. She held the figurine like a talisman, and it soothed the rage inside of her.

All around them, the water that shouldn't be there frothed red. Caleb caught glimpses of scaled limbs, teeth. A vast serpent encircling them. Tiamat. Jörmungandr. The World Snake. He remembered the names from Kyle's books.

The ground shuddered again. As if called by the blood spilled around him, Archie Royce sat up.

"Oh shit." Kyle took a step back, trying to pull Caleb with him.

Caleb dug his heels in. Rose edged toward them. Caleb caught her hand, pulled her close. Cere approached her father.

Archie turned his head. His hair stuck out wildly around his head, making Caleb think of a desiccated scarecrow left out too long in the rain. The terrible face in the sky had vanished with Del. Archie was only human now. Human and dead. Naked, pale, faced with the daughter he'd created.

Archie Royce looked small, pathetic.

Cere reached out and touched her father's face. Her palm covered it, her fingers stretching to his hairline. Every terrible thing inside her burned through her skin. Everything beautiful as well.

Archie screamed. The world flashed white hot, bringing a scent like a lightning-struck tree. Archie Royce's body collapsed, a pile of rot-softened flesh caving inward, so yellow-white bone protruded, ribs revealed to the sky. The mass juddered once, like he was still trying to wake, and fell still. The sky bulged, trying to rip itself apart. Cere closed her eyes.

Caleb reached for her, close enough to touch but miles apart. Finally his fingers brushed her hand. Her flesh was warm, hot, burning against his.

"I can't." Cere turned to him. Cracks riddled her eyes, gold light spilling through. Lines of char shot through her pale skin. "I can't stop it."

The earth shuddered. The sky opened along a bloody seam edged with teeth.

"Yes, you can."

Caleb let go of Kyle and Rose and threw his arms around Cere. If he could only hold onto her long enough, she wouldn't fall. She wouldn't jump. And maybe the world wouldn't end.

He tried to remember Catfish John's song, projecting it to her as she became smoke in his grasp, shadows. Too vast to hold. Tendrils of darkness lashed around him. Mouths filled with jagged teeth, dozens of mismatched eyes.

"I won't let go," Caleb shouted.

All at once, Cere was human again, small and sharp-boned in his arms, tears on her cheeks, drying instantly from the heat of her skin.

Caleb pressed his forehead against hers. His cheeks were wet too.

"Give me the darkness. Let it go."

"No." Cere's voice hitched. She tried to pull away. Caleb tightened his grip.

"Us," Rose said, stepping up beside him.

She wrapped her arms around Cere as well. Then Kyle was there too. They enclosed her, close enough to feel her pulse. Her body shuddered.

"No." Barely a whisper.

"Let us help you."

Caleb closed his eyes. He called Catfish John's song to mind again, letting it pour through him. Strange stars, cool water. Home.

A knot inside Cere let go. The darkness untangling. Cold stole Caleb's breath. Shadows lashed the sky. The stars peered at him. A burning wind howled through him. Everything all at once. The world ending and ending and ending, and dead faces in the water below the bridge crumbling. Kyle and Rose drowned. All the things he'd ever loved gone, and only hollow emptiness in its place.

Caleb threw back his head and screamed at the sky, a raw and painful sound. But he kept his arms around Cere, letting her hurt and loss into him.

Everything flared white again. The negative image of Cere against a rift of burning blackness opened in the sky. Walking away. At her side, a small figure no bigger than a child reached up a webbed hand to take hold of hers.

The stars blinked, black on white, and the world righted itself. When the ringing in his ears stopped, the first sound that returned was the cicadas. Caleb listened to them for what felt like a very long time, just trying to breathe.

Kyle and Rose's arms were still around him, but Cere was gone. Caleb's arms dropped to his side, his whole body heavy.

He looked at Kyle and Rose. Caleb could feel slivers of Cere's nightmares, flickering under his skin. He could see it in them too, haunting their eyes. How would he look at Rose at work from now on? What would he do the next time Kyle touched him?

Caleb pushed the thoughts away. A pile of bones lay nearby, stripped of flesh and aged beyond belief—all that remained of Archie Royce. Overhead, stars paled in a sky that had knit itself whole. Time had rolled back; the sun was just starting to rise.

"I think we did it, boss." Rose's voice was barely a whisper.

Caleb could only nod. Tears streamed down his cheeks, joy, relief, fear, everything. He didn't bother to wipe them away. He let them fall, and together, they watched as the sun climbed upward in the sky to set the top of the trees alight with a glorious new day.

chapter five

No one ever saw him leave. He was there and then gone. The only thing left were footprints, baked into the earth like they'd turned it to stone. Folks say he walked right off the edge of the earth, right into the sunset, waiting to be born again someday into a kinder world.

—*Myths, History, and Legends from the Delta to the Bayou* (Whippoorwill Press, 2016)

"So what happens now? You skipping town or what?" Rose glanced at Caleb and Kyle.

The three of them sat in chairs on the porch. Whether consciously or not, Caleb had brought a fourth chair out. It sat apart, and looking at it opened an aching space inside him.

They each held a mason jar of sweet tea, liberally spiked. Caleb propped his feet against the porch rail, leaning back.

"Still gunning for my job?" He tried to grin, but it felt stretched, flat.

"Wouldn't dream of it, boss."

Caleb turned his head toward Kyle. Right now, he was so tired the thought of going as far as the kitchen was exhausting, let alone the thought of leaving town. They hadn't talked about it, but he wondered. Kyle looked back at him, steady; Caleb could almost see him trying to process everything that had happened. It had been almost a week, but they both still woke up shivering, and Caleb couldn't help expecting to see Cere standing at the end of their bed every single time.

"What do you think?" Caleb asked softly.

Kyle started, coming back from a long way away. He frowned slightly and shook his head.

"I think it's something to talk about another day."

Caleb turned his attention back to Rose.

"What about you? Thinking about cutting out on me now that you've seen what kind of sheriff I make?"

"Nah. I think I'll stick right here. Besides, I owe you war stories." She said it lightly, but Caleb didn't miss the strain underneath her words.

Did she wake up with nightmares too? The thought pained him, but the idea of the dreams stopping was worse. Dreams meant the door was still open; there was still a chance Cere could come back. But if she did, what would she bring with her? Just because Del and Archie had been stopped, did that mean it was over? What if they hadn't done enough to save her?

The thoughts rolled around in his head without any answer. Kyle surprised him by taking his hand, lacing their fingers together.

"Think she'll ever come back?" Kyle asked.

Beside them, Rose sipped her tea, watching the sun go down, the sky turning all different shades of flame. If Caleb squinted, he could imagine a silhouette, very small against all the brightness. But he couldn't tell if it walked toward them or away.

"I don't know," he said, squeezing Kyle's hand.

It was the truth. He didn't know what the future held, but he and Kyle would figure it out together, and when it came to work, he and Rose would have each other's backs. The rest would fall into place.

And Cere, she was family. Whatever else might happen, no matter where they went, Caleb knew some part of him would always be waiting to welcome her home.

AC Wise was born and raised in Montreal and currently lives just far enough into the Philadelphia suburbs that deer roam her backyard. Her short fiction has appeared in publications such as *Shimmer*, *The Dark*, and *The Best Horror of the Year Volume Ten*, among other places. She has published two collections, *The Ultra Fabulous Glitter Squadron Saves the World Again* and *The Kissing Booth Girl and Other Stories*, the latter of which was a finalist for the Lambda Literary Award. Her story "The Last Sailing of the *Henry Charles Morgan* in Six Pieces of Scrimshaw (1841)" won the Sunburst Award for Excellence in Canadian Literature of the Fantastic. Find her online at www.acwise.net.

BROKEN EYE BOOKS

The Hole Behind Midnight, by Clinton J. Boomer
Crooked, by Richard Pett
Scourge of the Realm, by Erik Scott de Bie
Izanami's Choice, by Adam Heine
Never Now Always, by Desirina Boskovich
Pretty Marys All in a Row, by Gwendolyn Kiste
Queen of No Tomorrows, by Matt Maxwell
The Great Faerie Strike, by Spencer Ellsworth
Catfish Lullaby, by AC Wise

COLLECTIONS

Royden Poole's Field Guide to the 25th Hour, by Clinton J. Boomer

ANTHOLOGIES
(edited by Scott Gable & C. Dombrowski)
By Faerie Light: Tales of the Fair Folk
Ghost in the Cogs: Steam-Powered Ghost Stories
Tomorrow's Cthulhu: Stories at the Dawn of Posthumanity
Ride the Star Wind: Cthulhu, Space Opera, and the Cosmic Weird
Welcome to Miskatonic University: Fantastically Weird Tales of Campus Life
It Came from Miskatonic University: Weirdly Fantastical Tales of Campus Life
Nowhereville: Weird is Other People

Stay weird.
Read books.
Repeat.